SELF.
DESTRUCTED.

EVAN JACOBS

SADDLEBACK
PUBLISHING

GRAVEL ROAD

Bi-Normal
Edge of Ready
Falling Out of Place
I'm Just Me
Screaming Quietly
Self. Destructed.
2 Days
Unchained

SADDLEBACK
PUBLISHING
www.sdlback.com

ISBN-13: 978-1-62250-722-1
ISBN-10: 1-62250-722-3
eBook: 978-1-61247-973-6

Printed in Guangzhou, China
NOR/0414/CA21400666

18 17 16 15 14   1 2 3 4 5

Sometimes we find ourselves on a gravel road, not sure of how we got there or where the road leads. Sharp stones pellet the unprotected. And the everyday wear and tear sears more deeply.

ACKNOWLEDGEMENTS

While one person sits down to write a book, they are often influenced and informed by the people around them. They say it takes a village to raise a child. Well, it takes that many people to write a book sometimes.

I would like to thank Jeff Banks, Melisa De La Garza, Ed Harrison, Greg Stowers, Chris Lisk, and Robin Fry for their excellent contributions.

And of course I'd like to thank Shawn for being the best friend there is.

This book is also inspired by the music of Bruce Springsteen, Men at Work, Farside, Social Distortion, AC/DC,

Gameface, Underdog, Steely Dan, Harry Nilsson, the Who, Mavin Gaye, Black Flag, Naked Eyes, Face to Face, Sick of It All, Devo, A Chorus of Disapproval, Joy Division, Unbroken, the Rolling Stones, Judge, Eleven Thirty-Four, Motorhead, Pink Floyd, Outspoken, Snapcase, Minor Threat, the Descendents, Pearl Jam, Cro-Mags, and Dag Nasty.

ASHLEY

Nice shirt." Ashley Walters smiled as she passed Michael Ellis. She was paying a compliment to his T-shirt for the band the Who. It was the one where the *O* in the name had an arrow coming out of it, and there was a red, white, and blue bull's-eye behind it.

"You want it?" Michael replied looking up from his *MacWorld* magazine. Ashley laughed. Her smile was enough to let him know she thought he was okay; that he could keep talking to her.

"I'll give it you, seriously." Michael started to lift his shirt up, ignoring the fact that he was wearing a jacket. Realizing it would be impossible to take off, Michael stopped trying.

"Come on, keep going." Ashley's smile became a stern expression. "You *did* offer."

Michael stared at her. Ashley had really inviting hazel eyes. They went well with her dark complexion and thick brown hair. She wore a pair of white tennis shoes, white shorts, and a red T-shirt.

"Okay, I'll let you off the hook." She smiled. "I can see by your jacket that you run for the school. Running's cool."

"You like to run?" Michael asked.

Ashley nodded her head.

"You want to run together sometime?" He asked the question before he realized what he was saying.

"You think you can keep up with me?" She jogged in place. "I'm pretty fast."

"I run the hundred-yard dash."

"Wow, that's a humble brag." She smiled.

Michael liked how she teased him and seemed interested at the same time.

"You're new here," Michael stated.

"Do I stand out that much?"

"In a good way."

Michael had no idea why he was saying all these things. There was something about Ashley. He felt drawn to her. She didn't seem like the other girls at Willmore High School. He felt like it was okay to talk with her like this.

"Well, I've gotta run. Not literally." She smiled again. Dazzling. "But you better stay in training. Especially if you're gonna keep up when you take me running."

"Okay."

"I'm Ashley."

"Michael."

He wanted to set up a time for their run but she was gone.

Michael thought about going after her but he didn't. He had a feeling he would be talking to her again. He just didn't know when, which kind of bothered him.

John walked up. He was wearing the same Willmore High School track jacket that Michael was wearing. It said Willmore across the back and had a runner in the center.

"Who was that girl you were talking to?" John asked.

"That was Ashley."

"She's cute."

Michael continued to watch Ashley as she walked away. Eventually, she blended into the crowd of students.

The school year had basically just started, and Michael thought it was gonna be a great one.

MICHAEL

Michael jogged home after track practice. There was a bus he could've taken with a group of other students, but Michael preferred running.

"I like running to school and running home," he told people. "It helps me clear my head."

He'd been running to and from Willmore since he started there as a freshman. He was a junior now.

The area that he and the other students were bused from was just outside the town of Willmore. It was called Porterville. It was also considered the "poorer" section.

(Some of the rich Willmore students called it "Poorerville.") The homes, parks, and stores were all older. The high school that had initially been there was torn down, so all the students in the area went to the newer one in Willmore.

Michael's friends John and Kevin were also from Porterville, but they took the bus unless John got to use his parents' car.

Michael's thoughts turned to his homework. He had seven classes. The first week of school was over, and the teachers were starting to pile it on. Michael didn't mind; he just wished he was better at English. It wasn't that he didn't like the subject; it just wasn't concrete and simple to him like math and science. Too many gray areas.

"There are so many ways to look at this stuff," he once told a teacher. "It confuses me because I never know if I'm looking at it the right way."

Michael wanted to be a pediatrician.

He had two older brothers, Erik and Jason. They were both married with kids. Michael got along well with all of them. Jason had a girl, Ally, who was six. Erik had two boys, Kyle and Sebastian, who were seven and nine.

One time Michael was watching all the kids. Sebastian fell. He skinned his knee and it bled a lot. Michael patched Sebastian up. Sebastian was crying, and Michael made him feel better. He liked how that felt. That's what made him want to help children.

As he neared his home, he ran past Otis Park. It was really run-down. There were two rusty swings and one sorry slide. Next to that was a basketball court with rusted hoops and a large patch of brown grass. When Michael was younger, he'd loved going there. For a while.

One time when he was six, his brothers were babysitting him. They thought it would be funny to take him to the park and leave him there. Michael tried to find his way home, but he got lost. The farther he walked, the more scared and lost he got.

Eventually, a neighbor spotted him wandering around crying, and they helped him find his way home.

His mom comforted him like she always did.

"It's okay now," she said as she kissed his forehead. "Everything's going to be fine, sweetie."

His dad yelled at his brothers, but he seemed disappointed in Michael. As if he, at six years old, should have known how to get home on his own.

THE SETUP

No invite?" Ashley called as Michael ran around the perimeter of the Willmore track field.

It's her, he said to himself and stopped running.

Michael walked over to Ashley. She was hanging out by the fence, standing next to two popular girls, who were both talking on their cell phones. Their names were Blanca and Tori. They were rich girls that Michael had never really talked to. He assumed Ashley was with them.

Ashley was wearing jeans and a white hoodie. Her brown hair hung down her back in a ponytail. Michael felt himself breathing heavier and heavier.

"I'm sorry." Michael grinned.

"You run before practice?" Ashley asked, motioning to the other runners who were all stretching.

"Yeah. I stretch too ... I just, I like running." He was hoping he didn't sound weird. Michael always found that people liked him, but sometimes they thought he was odd. Like running before track practice. He did things he didn't need to do. "Did you move here over the summer?" he asked.

"Yeah, with my parents. My dad's a doctor at the hospital. The main one in Willmore."

"I want to be a doctor."

"Really?"

"Yeah." Michael wiped some sweat from his brow. He hoped he wasn't sweating too much. His breathing had steadied.

"I want to work with kids. What about you? What do you want to do when you graduate?"

"I like writing. I want to do something with that."

"I wish I was better at writing. I like math and science."

"I'm not surprised."

"Really?" Michael asked, confused. "Why?"

"You seem smart. Really smart people always like math and science better than English."

"I've never thought about it like that," Michael replied. He wasn't sure he understood what Ashley meant, but he was pretty sure she wasn't messing with him.

She doesn't know me well enough to do that, he thought.

"So does that mean I'm smarter than you?" After he said it, Michael realized he might have offended her.

"You might be. At least you like good music." Ashley just seemed to go with the flow. Michael thought she liked talking to him.

"I also like movies," Michael stated.

"Me too."

"What's your favorite one?"

"I like the *Harry Potter* ones."

"Me too. I liked the first one the best, though." Michael had seen all the *Harry Potter* movies.

"I loved them all," Ashley said.

Then there was a lull in the conversation. This sometimes happened to him. It was hard to keep a conversation going, especially when he was nervous.

I wish I could kiss you, he thought. *Would she let me kiss her sometime?*

"Were you serious about going running with me?" Michael knew he should have been more forceful. John and his other friends told him that you never "ask" a girl to do anything. You "tell" her what she's going to do.

Michael couldn't do that.

"Were *you* serious? I think you're afraid you'll see how good I am, and then you'll lose your spot on the team." Ashley laughed after she said that.

She laughs a lot after she says things, but she's not laughing at me, Michael told himself. *I think she just thinks a lot of things are funny.*

"Let's go running on Saturday night." Michael put it out there. This was the hang-fire moment.

"That sounds like a date." She eyed him coyly.

"Maybe it is." Michael smiled.

Now it's my turn to laugh. And he did.

"Okay."

Ashley wrote down her phone number and gave it to him.

Michael stuffed the paper into his

pocket just as Blanca and Tori were getting off their phones. He gave Ashley a quick smile as he heard the coach blow his whistle for the start of practice.

As Michael ran back to the team, he wondered what Blanca and Tori might tell Ashley about him. They'd known Michael since freshman year. Would they make fun of Ashley for dating a guy from Poorerville?

Don't worry about that, he told himself. *You're going out with Ashley, not them.*

MEET THE
PARENTS

Hey, come on in, Mike," Ashley's dad said as he extended his hand. Michael shook it as he walked into Ashley's big two-story house. Normally, he didn't like being called "Mike," but he wasn't going to tell that to Ashley's dad.

The house had hardwood floors, leather couches, modern light fixtures. Everything was new. It also had a dramatic entrance with a winding staircase in the middle of the house.

This looks like something out of a movie, Michael thought.

This was in stark contrast to Michael's house. It had older carpet, older furniture, and "popcorn" ceilings. His parents worked hard to make it look nice, but they didn't have enough money to do a lot of improvements.

"Ashley tells me you want to be a doctor," her father said as they sat in the living room.

"Yeah. A pediatrician," Michael stated.

"That's admirable. It's a very a competitive field. You've got to get into a good school. You need to be an ace student. Everything. A good doctor has to be top-notch."

Her father eyed Michael as he picked up his drink off the table. It was almost like he was asking, "Are you top-notch, Michael? Are you good enough for my daughter?"

Ashley's mom walked out with a big smile on her face. She looked like Ashley, only older. They had the same long brown hair. The same warm, inviting hazel eyes.

"Hi, Michael," Ashley's mother shook his hand as he stood up. "Can I get you something to drink?"

"No, thank you," he said. Michael wanted to make a good impression. He wanted Ashley's parents to like him and to tell her that he'd make a good boyfriend.

Ashley walked downstairs dressed in pink sweats and a white hoodie.

"I thought we were going running?" She smiled.

Michael was wearing dark blue jeans and a white button-down shirt. He hadn't forgotten. They were some of the nicest clothes he had. He didn't want to meet her parents wearing sweats.

"Oh, Ashley," her mother started, "you're not going out like that?"

"Yeah, we're going to the best restaurant in town, right, Michael?" Ashley eyed him.

"Well …" Michael had to think fast. "I'm going there. You might have some problems getting in."

That made Ashley's parents laugh.

"So you don't want to run?" Ashley asked. "You know what? Let's get pizza. I know a great place," she said. Before Michael could respond, Ashley disappeared up the stairs.

"That's Ashley," her mother said as she walked out of the room.

"Yeah, she's a girl who knows what she wants." As her father said that, he eyed Michael. The way he said it was odd.

Is he questioning why she might want me?

He talked with Ashley's father for a few more minutes before she came back down wearing jeans, a T-shirt, and her white hoodie.

Then they left the house. Michael wasn't able to stop questioning everything Ashley's father had said.

Does he like me? Does he not like me?

Michael told himself to relax. He was with Ashley now, and that was who he really cared about.

FIRST DATE

Michael and Ashley went to Arrighi's Pizza Shack. The pizza was really good, but Michael hardly remembered eating it.

From the moment they left Ashley's house, they talked non-stop. About school, their friends, growing up, their mutual love of classic rock music. Everything.

After they ate, they continued walking and talking. Michael told her about his brothers and their kids. Ashley told Michael about the stories she liked to write.

"My friends tease me because sometimes I won't hang out so I can stay home and write." She laughed.

That laugh. Michael loved it.

"You're not afraid to be different," he told her.

"Why would I be?" she asked. "Different is better than being normal. I like different. You're different. That's way more interesting than following the crowd."

Is she saying she likes me? He was dying to ask her. He'd been wondering all night. She had said all the right things. All the things that a guy would want to hear.

I think she likes being with me. No ... I know she does, he kept telling himself. It made him less nervous.

Five hours after the date began, Michael and Ashley found themselves back in front of her house. Since they started heading home, his nervousness had returned.

Should I kiss her? Will she let me kiss

her? Am I expected to kiss her? He kept going back and forth.

Eventually, they were on the front porch.

"We really covered a lot of ground tonight," she said.

"It was awesome."

"I had a great time." She smiled warmly.

Michael glanced at her house and saw her father watching them from the window. He was sitting in a chair, holding a magazine, but he kept looking up at them.

"We'll do this again," Michael said.

Ashley gave him a hug. "Yeah … well, wear your running stuff next time."

She smiled at him and started walking inside.

You idiot! he told himself. *You should've kissed her right then. Who cares if her dad was watching?*

"See you Monday," she said from the door.

"Yeah."

"You're supposed to say 'Not if I see you first.' " Ashley laughed.

"Not if I see you first." Michael smiled.

They locked eyes just before the door closed shut.

REALITY
CHECK

Michael and Ashley talked on the phone every day after that. Sometimes the conversation lasted thirty minutes, other times it was three hours. At school they made plans to hang out on Friday.

"Just admit it, Michael," John said as they played *Call of Duty* with Kevin on his Xbox. They were hanging out at John's house after practice on Thursday.

"I like her," Michael said, wishing the conversation had never turned to Ashley.

He'd talked about girls with his friends before, but he never felt about them the way he did about Ashley.

This girl isn't like any girl I've ever known, he thought. *She can do anything she wants ... And it seems like she wants to be with me.*

Ashley made Michael comfortable with being himself. She gave him confidence.

No person had ever really given him that before.

"I wonder what she wants," Kevin asked.

Michael looked at John as he and Kevin continued to play the video game. The electronic battle sounds surrounded them.

"What do you mean?" Michael asked. He started to feel the inside of his stomach get cold.

"What?" Kevin asked, looking at Michael.

"Why would Ashley want anything?" Michael felt himself starting to get angry.

"Because she's hanging out with you." Kevin laughed.

Kevin looked at John. John tried to hide his smirk, but he couldn't.

"Why wouldn't she hang out with me?" Michael wasn't going to let this go. "Ashley has been hanging out with me every day since our first date. She obviously likes me ... why would she want something from me?"

"You haven't even kissed her. If she liked you so much, why wouldn't she let you do that?" Kevin continued to play the video game, dismissing Michael. "Just being real, Mikey. Maybe you're one of her projects."

"What are you talking about? You don't even know her!" Michael yelled defensively. "And don't call me that!"

He stood up so quickly it startled John and Kevin.

"I can't believe you two. You don't even know me! Forget you guys if you think she wants something from me.

"When was the last time either of you went on a date? You losers just sit here playing video games. I don't see girls knocking down your door. So shut your mouths!"

Michael turned and stormed out.

AGAINST
ALL ODDS

Michael's fast walk soon turned into a run. He thought running would make him feel better.

Michael headed in the direction of Ashley's house. He had driven there on their first date.

"I just need to go somewhere once," he told people. "Then I can always go back without directions."

Michael was about a mile from Ashley's house. He slowed his pace to a fast walk. His breathing was heavy, but it wasn't from the run. He took out his phone.

"Hello?" Ashley asked when she answered her phone.

"Can we meet?" Michael asked. *I hope I don't sound too desperate,* he thought.

"Now?" Ashley laughed.

"Yeah. If you can ..." Michael was nervous that she wouldn't be able to meet him. He *had* to see her. Now.

"Sure," Ashley replied, as if Michael's urgency had come through the phone.

LAYING IT ON THE LINE

Ashley met Michael at a park near her house.

Why didn't she have me come inside? I could've said hello to her parents. Is she embarrassed of me? Maybe Kevin's right … maybe I'm just one of her projects.

Michael told himself to block out those thoughts. He was upset enough. He didn't want to scare Ashley off by appearing frantic.

I have to tell her how I feel. I have to kiss her … he told himself. *Even though*

I don't have her ... I don't want to lose her. If I'm too friendly, all she'll ever see me as is a friend.

"So I'm not even sure if they're gonna run my story." Ashley was telling Michael about an article she had written about broken lockers for the school newspaper. "I'm like, 'Why did you tell me to write the story if you didn't want it?' "

"Yeah," Michael said. He stared straight ahead.

"Is everything okay?" she asked him.

"Yeah." He tried to smile.

"No, it's not. What's the matter? When you called you sounded like you *had* to see me."

Michael stared into her beautiful hazel eyes. He was so nervous. He felt himself starting to shake.

"I did," he practically choked the words out. "I had to see you."

"How come?" Ashley's expression

became concerned. "Are you okay?"

"Yeah ... I just. I like you, Ashley. A lot. And I'm scared that if I don't tell you, I'll never tell you. I love being around you. I love hearing you talk. I can't wait to hear what you're gonna say next. I can spend time with you, and we don't have to do anything. Just being with you is enough." Michael was breathing heavy after he said those words. He was shaking. He didn't know what to do next.

He closed his eyes and kissed Ashley.

Not too hard. Stop breathing so fast.

And then Ashley wrapped her arms softly around his neck.

She's kissing you back!

Michael wrapped his arms around her.

And for the first time since he left John and Kevin, for the first time in a long time, Michael wasn't thinking about anything.

THE BOSS

I'm Going Down" by Bruce Springsteen was playing as Michael was getting ready. He was going to a dance Friday night at the high school.

Michael stared at himself in the mirror as he combed his hair.

Do you think you're a good-looking guy? he asked himself. *You must be if Ashley's with you.*

They had hung out even more after their first kiss. They hadn't gone too far beyond that, but Michael was happy with where they were.

I think she thinks of me as her boy-friend. He didn't want to think too much about it. It was hard because he liked knowing where he stood with people.

As long as I'm the only person she's dating. She's the only person I want to date ... I think we're basically boyfriend and girlfriend.

He eyed a CD he had made her of all his favorite songs.

She's gonna love it.

"Don't you look handsome," his mom said as he was walking out of the house.

His parents were sitting in the living room. The front door of the house opened up into it.

His dad had never been particularly emotional with Michael or his brothers. Once he was made manager at the call center where he worked, he became even more removed.

"I have to work with kids who are the same age as my own sons," his dad would complain to his mom.

"I hope Ashley thinks I look nice," Michael said shyly.

"She will." His mom beamed. "I'm so happy that you think you've found somebody."

It gave Michael a lot of pride to have a girlfriend. To be able to show his parents that he was somebody that a person outside his family could like. That he was normal.

"It's great to care for someone, Michael," his dad said as he eyed the TV. His parents were watching a game show; they watched them all the time. "But you need to stay focused. You're really smart. You make good marks. You can't always count on that to get you through. You've gotta work hard. Always. You graduate next year. You're gonna take your SATs next semester. Don't get so involved with this girl that you can't think straight."

His dad looked at him after he said that.

"I won't," Michael said.

He knew that he was really into Ashley. Maybe more than he should've been for somebody in a new relationship.

Don't think about it, Michael kept telling himself as he drove his mom's car over to Ashley's house. *Just have a good time tonight. Take things one day at a time.*

ODD MAN OUT

Even though Michael had blocked out his talk with his dad, he was still having an off night.

It began with Ashley's father. As he waited in the front room of Ashley's house, he was surprised that Ashley's dad didn't ask him to sit down.

"Going to the dance tonight?" her father asked.

"Yeah. A bunch of us are going together."

"Enjoy this now …" Her father smiled. "You'll be saying good-bye to your social life if you get into medical school."

"I am going to get into medical school." Michael hoped he didn't sound defiant. There was something in Ashley's dad's tone that bothered him.

He makes me feel like I always have to defend myself.

"I went to Stanford," Ashley's father said. He stared directly into Michael's eyes. He stared so hard it seemed like he was trying to stare through him. "You have any thoughts on where you want to go?"

"I want to go to UCSD." Michael stared at Ashley's father. He didn't say anything. "I'd like to go to Stanford, but that place costs a lot more money."

"Yes, Michael, it does. However, I felt it was worth it because I wanted to be the best in my field."

Ashley's friends were less than cordial to Michael on the ride over to the school.

It wasn't anything they said. It was what they didn't say that bothered him. It was as if Michael wasn't even there.

He knew they didn't think he was as good as they were. But it bothered him that they did it so flippantly.

They make me feel like I'm nothing, he thought. *Like I'm not as cool or as good as them. They think I'm poor because of where I live.*

Michael stared out the window of the car. He looked at all the big houses in Willmore. They made his house look like a shack.

Suddenly, Michael felt Ashley's hand in his. He looked into her eyes. She smiled and squeezed his hand.

At that moment, Michael completely surrendered himself emotionally.

She believes in me. I've never been as

comfortable as I am around Ashley. I've never felt like this about anybody.

Ashley kissed him slowly on the lips. Normally this might have embarrassed Michael. He felt weird about public displays of affection. But it didn't bother him at all with Ashley.

It just feels right, he thought as they continued to kiss. *Everything with Ashley is perfect.*

Her friends weren't talking to Michael, but they were probably watching him now.

GUNS

That Sunday Michael was dusting and vacuuming the house. Aside from mowing the lawn, it was the only real chore his parents gave him.

He'd gone to church with them. After that, Michael wanted to stay home in case Ashley called and wanted to do something.

They'd danced a little bit that night, but mainly they spent their time talking.

"It was a great time," Ashley said at the end of the night.

As Michael moved the vacuum, he kept running things Ashley said over in his mind.

I like you because you're different. That was the one comment that stuck out the most to Michael.

She accepts me for who I am. Totally.

Michael had vacuumed the living room and bedrooms. Now he was in his dad's study. In it was a large desk, a nice leather chair, and a bunch of books. His dad had his degree in communications framed on the wall. There were pictures of the grand-kids. And his father's gun case.

The guns hung on the wall. There were six of them. Handguns. There was a lock on the case.

Michael vacuumed the room. Then he was going to dust. He always saved the gun display for last.

"I don't like them," he had told his brothers when he was younger. "I can see why people do ... they look powerful."

As Michael sprayed cleaner on the

glass display, he suddenly had a thought. And it wasn't about Ashley.

It was about her friends.

And her father.

If I walked around with one of these guns in a holster, I'll bet they wouldn't be so high-minded, Michael thought. *Ashley's dad would probably show me a lot more respect.*

Michael laughed to himself after that.

Then the thought was gone.

I could never carry a gun, he told himself.

SIGNALS
CROSSED

I loved the comp you made for me," Ashley said as she and Michael were walking home from school Thursday afternoon. It had rained almost all day. The track coach canceled practice because the track was so wet. Michael had been walking Ashley home almost every day that week.

She had come to his track meet on Tuesday. Michael had won his race. Ashley kissed him when the events were over. She had done it in front of everybody.

It wasn't a long kiss, but it was long enough. Just thinking about it made Michael feel good. *Having Ashley there was better than winning. It was better than every win I've ever had.*

Michael's thoughts turned to the upcoming weekend.

I need to make plans for tomorrow, he told himself. Michael figured eventually he wouldn't feel the need to make definitive plans with Ashley. It would just become something that was happening. Until then, he wasn't taking any chances.

"I can make you another mix for tomorrow night," Michael offered. He hoped that would be a subtle enough suggestion to get something going.

"What if I planned on making you one?" Ashley asked.

So she's already thinking about seeing me again to give me something. Michael sighed slightly.

He knew he was worrying for nothing. He knew that Ashley liked him … he just liked knowing it. There was another dance coming up in a few weeks. It was nothing special, but Michael really wanted them to go together.

"In fact," Ashley took her iPod out of her bag. "Maybe you can help me."

"Sure," he responded.

Ashley scrolled through her long list of songs. She found "Satisfaction" by the Rolling Stones.

"That's a good one," Michael said.

Ashley continued scrolling. She stopped on "Reeling in the Years" by Steely Dan.

"You're just knocking them out of the park, Ash." Michael put his arm around her and she smiled.

I love your smile, he thought. He'd told her that before, but it didn't seem appropriate to say now.

Ashley continued flipping around.

She landed on "Baby" by Justin Bieber.

"You probably love that song," she joked.

Michael stared at the screen. Ashley started to flip through the songs again.

"Why do you have that song?" His tone was flat.

"I used to like it. Let's see … what other classic stuff do I have on here?" She kept searching her iPod.

"Why would you like that song? It's terrible."

She looked at Michael. Her face was stern, without a laugh behind it.

"Yeah, it's stupid, but whatever. I like a lot of music."

"Even stuff like that? It's so fake and shallow." Just like when they first met, Michael was saying things without thinking. He couldn't stop himself. Only this time he wasn't making Ashley laugh.

"Is it really that big of a deal? You need to lighten up, Michael." Ashley continued to have her stern expression.

I wish she'd smile. Then I could make her laugh, or she could make me laugh, Michael told himself.

"No … it's just," Michael was searching for the right words. He just couldn't find them. "That music's so *fake*. You're not fake at all, Ashley. Only fake people listen to that kind of music. I just … I thought you knew that."

Then Ashley's stern expression softened. She didn't smile, though. Her look was one of indifference.

"Well," she started, "I guess I'm fake, then."

"But you're not …" He almost laughed. "You're not like Blanca and Tori. I wonder sometimes why you hang out with them."

"I *like* them."

"Why?"

"I don't know. Why do you like your friends?"

Michael was really flustered. He had never had a conversation like this with her. It wasn't even a conversation. It was like they were fighting.

"Let's just stop talking about it," Ashley said when Michael didn't respond.

They walked the rest of the way home in silence.

I don't know what to say, Michael kept telling himself. He was hoping something would change by the time they got to her house. But it didn't. There was a lot of tension.

When they got there, Ashley said bye. Then she went into her house without even giving Michael a hug.

COLD
FEELINGS

Michael didn't sleep at all that night. He was fighting a rising panic. He would've called Ashley, but he thought it might be better to let her cool down.

I don't want her to think I'm smothering her.

Every time he started to doze off, he would wake up. He had a cold feeling running through his body. But he didn't sleep. He curled up in a ball under his blanket.

Why did I say those things? he wondered. *Why didn't I just let it go? I know Ashley ... I know she's not fake.*

All of these thoughts and ideas were floating around in his head. They made him feel sick and afraid. They made him feel how he felt that time his brothers left him in the park.

Am I alone again? he kept asking himself. *I have to talk to her. I have to hear her voice. I have to know she's not mad at me. That everything's okay."*

Eventually, morning came.

And then ... Michael realized that because of their argument, he'd never made plans with Ashley for that night. Friday night. They always made plans.

CHANGES

Michael ran to school early the next morning. The run only made him feel slightly better. He tried to call Ashley once he got there, but she didn't pick up her phone.

After his first two classes, Michael thought he might see her at break. He didn't. Then he thought he might see her at lunch. Not there either.

Is she hiding from me? Trying to prove a point?

"You wanna roll with us after practice?" John asked as he and Michael were standing on the field.

Michael was listlessly looking around

for Ashley. He scanned the fence, hoping he might see her standing there. She'd be smiling at him and say something like, "Are you over that song now? Justin Bieber is just as big as Led Zeppelin was in their time." Or something just as sassy to let Michael know it was no big deal.

But she wasn't there.

Eventually, practice started. Michael realized that she wasn't going to show up. He was going to be alone for the first Friday since they had started hanging out.

He hated it. But it wasn't the first time he'd pushed people away because he couldn't let things go.

FRIDAY
LET ME DOWN

Michael sat at the dinner table staring at his food. He had barely eaten anything.

"You want some more bread?" his mom asked his dad.

"No," his father said in between bites.

This isn't how my Friday is supposed to be, Michael thought. *I'm supposed to be with Ashley, talking. My parents don't talk. My mom asks my dad things, and he gives her answers. They don't mean anything.*

"You're gonna have a lot more girl-friends, Michael," his father suddenly said.

His parents had obviously taken notice of the fact that Michael was home on Friday night. He hadn't been dating Ashley for long, but it was long enough to be noticed. "At your age I was smart enough to never go for just one girl. Besides, you've got a lot to think about with college and your future. How's studying for the SATs going?"

"Haven't started," Michael said in a dull tone. He wanted to be anywhere but here.

"You better get started. Those tests can make or break your college prospects."

College? SATs? I'll get those sorted out once I work things out with Ashley, he told himself.

"Okay," Michael finally said to his dad.

He couldn't talk to him. His dad wouldn't understand how he felt about Ashley. His mom might, though.

I'd feel weird talking to my mom about a girl.

TOO MUCH,
TOO LATE

Saturday morning, Michael got Ashley on the phone.

"Tori and I went to the movies," Ashley said, explaining why she wasn't with Michael the night before.

It was supposed to be our date night, he told himself.

"What'd you see?" he asked.

"The *Place Beyond the Pines*," she replied.

That's the new Ryan Gosling movie. She probably likes him. I wouldn't stand a chance if Ashley had a choice between him and me.

They continued talking, but their conversation was stale. There were awkward gaps and pauses.

"Wanna hang out tonight?" Michael asked. He stopped breathing for a moment.

"I can't."

"Why not?"

"I have plans with Blanca and a few other friends." Ashley's tone was cool.

Is she really gonna punish me like this because I don't like a Justin Bieber song? Michael was starting to get angry.

"I'd invite you," Ashley continued. "But I know you don't like them."

"That's because they don't like me," Michael shot back.

He expected her to tell him he was wrong. That her friends *did* like him. That she liked him, and that they were going to get past their argument.

But Ashley didn't say that.

"Can we hang out next Friday?" he asked. Again, he stopped breathing.

"Yeah, that should work." But there was no sweetness in Ashley's voice. No sassiness followed by her reassuring laugh.

Michael felt like he was talking her into doing something she really didn't want to do.

Eventually, they got off the phone.

Michael realized he'd never apologized for getting so upset at her. He thought about calling her back but didn't feel like he could.

THIRD PERSON
PARANOIA

The next few weeks were weird for Michael. He and Ashley continued to talk at school and on the phone, but she would only hang out with him at school.

Even then, he thought, *we barely talk for that long because we don't have time.*

She even canceled their Friday plans that she had told him should work.

All their conversations were about their classes or something that had happened on campus that day.

Whenever I bring up hanging out, she says, "Let me get back to you about that." It's like she won't forgive me for what I said.

Ashley wasn't answering her phone when Michael called either.

About two weeks after the "Bieber" incident, even their time chatting at school started to get shorter.

"Where's your girl?" John asked one day as he was going off campus for lunch.

"She's with the Key Club," Michael said.

Michael had been in that organization when he was a freshman. Then he decided he'd rather hang out with his friends at lunch instead.

"A lot of students do that because it looks good when you apply to college," he added.

THROUGH THE GRAPEVINE

So are you cool about Ashley?" Kevin asked.

He was sitting in the passenger seat of John's car. Michael was in the back. Normally he would run home, but it was raining. John rarely got to drive his parents' car, but today he was—probably because of the rain.

"What do you mean?" Michael was surprised Kevin had brought her up. After he insulted him at John's house, Michael didn't talk about her with him.

"She's with Scott Hicks now."

Michael felt a searing pain in the pit of his stomach. Then the cold feeling he'd had since the fight with Ashley doubled in strength.

Scott Hicks, Michael thought. *He's a football player. He lives in a big house right across the street from Willmore High School. Right near Ashley.*

Michael was getting so worked up, he was shaking. He couldn't stop.

"Are you okay, Michael?" John looked at him from the rearview mirror.

Michael couldn't answer. He kept staring at John's head.

"These things happen, bro," Kevin went on. "You'll meet somebody else. You should come to my brother's party on Saturday."

He's just talking, Michael told himself, seething. *He's just saying things that everybody says. I don't want another girl.*

I want Ashley. I want things to be how they were.

John's car came to a red light.

John and Kevin were talking. Michael was so upset he couldn't even hear them. He saw their lips moving, but all he heard was a pounding in his ears.

He unbuckled his seat belt, opened the door, and got out.

"Where are you going?" John yelled. Kevin was laughing.

Michael paid no attention to the traffic as he walked through it. Cars honked at him. Driver's yelled. But he paid them no mind. He was numb.

THE
REAL ME

Hey, you've reached Ashley," the message on her voice mail said.

Michael hung up the phone. He didn't know how many times he had heard this message, but he was sick of it.

As he approached her house, Michael saw Ashley run out the front door. She was headed toward their driveway where her mom waited in the running car.

"Ashley!" Michael yelled as he ran toward her.

Just as Ashley was about to open the

car door, she stopped and turned.

"Michael," she said, startled.

Something in her voice made Michael stop abruptly. Ashley moved toward him, and he thought she might give him a hug.

"What are you doing here?"

He had so much he wanted to say to her. Michael looked and saw her mom watching them from the car.

She isn't turning off the car. She thinks this is going to be quick. Ashley will tell me that it's over, and then I'll be gone. That thought made Michael even angrier.

"So this is it?" Michael stated. "You're with Scott Hicks now? You couldn't even tell me."

"Michael," Ashley sighed. For the first time since their argument, Michael saw kindness in her face again. "We were never really together. We were just dating."

"Ashley …" Michael was trying to be

as calm as possible. "I'm sorry about that song. I'm sorry about what I said about your friends. You can't really be ending this because of that."

"It's not because of that, Michael. I like you a lot. As a friend."

"Do you make out with your friends? Were you with him the whole time? Was I just a joke to you?" Michael shrieked.

Ashley's mom turned off the car. Ashley looked over at her.

"You're a fake! You're everything you said you're not!" Michael yelled.

The door to the house opened. Ashley's dad ran out and got between them.

"Michael," he said in a stern tone. "If you don't leave, I'm calling the police."

"Sir." Again Michael tried to calm down. He didn't know if he'd have a chance like this again. "I know you feel threatened by me. She's you're daughter, and you think I'm gonna take her away …"

Michael couldn't control himself. He lunged at Ashley, wanting to plead his case. Her father grabbed him and threw him to the ground.

"This is your last warning, Michael!" her father was towering over him now. "I'm going to call the police. I mean it. Stay away from Ashley."

"You'd never do this to Scott Hicks, would you?" Michael screamed.

He got to his feet, and both Ashley and her father took a few steps back.

Then Michael stared into Ashley's eyes.

She still cares about me. She still wants to be with me. I know it. She's just confused right now. Her father. Scott. Everybody's messed her up.

He stared at Ashley for a second longer. Then he turned and ran away. He didn't want to give Ashley's father the satisfaction of seeing him cry.

GO SOLO

Michael sat with John and Kevin. They were talking, but he wasn't paying attention. He watched as some students removed posters from the recent dance.

I didn't even get a chance to take her, he thought. *It wasn't anything special, but it mattered to me.*

It was just one more thing to regret about his relationship with Ashley.

Then, as if on cue, he saw Ashley and Scott walking across the campus.

Could I ever be part of her world? he wondered. *They see me as poor and less than them. I thought I was special to her, but it was all in my head.*

"Forget about her, Michael," John said as he looked around the campus.

Michael didn't say anything.

I can't, he told himself. *And nothing anybody says is going to make me. I'm not gonna forget about Ashley Walters until I'm ready.*

OVERKILL

Halloween had come and gone. Michael's friends all went to a party. He stayed home, passed out candy, and hung out in his room.

"I don't even feel like watching scary movies," he told his mom. Michael had talked with her a little about Ashley but not much. *She doesn't get it. She just tells me "there's other fish in the sea," but none of that helps me now.*

Thanksgiving was always one of Michael's favorite holidays. He loved hanging out with his brothers. Michael especially loved seeing their kids.

It wasn't like that at all this year.

Michael played the Wii for a while with his nephews, but he couldn't stop thinking about what Ashley might be doing.

As he watched his brothers interact with their wives, Michael kept wondering if that was how he and Ashley could've been.

Is there any way we could still have that?

Then he had a thought he'd had more times than he could count.

She's going to realize that Scott isn't right for her. She has to. And when she does, I'll be there. And she'll remember why she liked me in the first place.

After barely eating anything at dinner, Michael's brothers cornered him in their father's study. It was hard, but Michael opened up to them about Ashley and everything that had happened.

"You're gonna have problems with women all your life," Erik said.

"Look at us." Jason smiled. "We're married, and we still have problems with them."

Both brothers laughed. This only increased Michael's frustration.

"You guys don't understand. This isn't a joke." Michael's voice was loud.

His brother's stared at him.

They look confused, Michael thought. *They have no idea who I am.*

He must've been louder than he thought. Because suddenly his dad appeared behind Jason and Erik.

"How many times have I told you to forget about that girl?" his father barked. "Michael, you need to stop being a baby about this and act like a man."

Embarrassed and beginning to feel his eyes well up, Michael stormed off to his bedroom. He heard his father grumbling about his behavior. Then his dad changed the subject and started to talk to Michael's brothers about some of the guns in the case.

Michael dropped facedown on his bed and cried into his pillow. His stomach hurt; he was so cold inside. After a few moments his mom came in. She sat next to him and ran her hand through his hair.

"It's gonna be okay, sweetheart," she kept saying. "You'll meet somebody else. Somebody who really loves you. First loves always break your heart. It will get better."

"Ashley loves me," Michael managed to squeeze out through his tears. "I know she does."

"I know, I know …" his mom said. She continued to run her hand through his hair. Eventually, she left Michael alone. The pain he was in now was even more intense. He never felt so miserable.

IT'S A
MISTAKE

It was really hot on the Willmore campus during lunch.

Michael had been going off campus to eat with John.

The less I'm on the campus, the better, he told himself. *It's just too hard seeing Ashley with Scott.*

That day John was broke, so they stayed at school.

A bunch of students were having a water balloon fight. Normally the campus security would stop it. Since it was contained to one area, nobody seemed to mind. Or at least be paying attention.

Ashley and Scott were in the center of the fight, laughing and having fun. They were working as a team, trying to soak Tori, Blanca, and the rest of their friends.

Michael sat across the quad, watching. He was transfixed.

She's moved on from me. She doesn't even care. It's like I'm not even here.

Suddenly, a water balloon slammed into his chest.

"Got you!" John laughed and ran off.

Michael smiled slightly. He looked around and spotted a tub of water sitting on a patch of grass. There were three forgotten water balloons floating in it.

Michael grabbed one and moved over to where most of the students were playing.

As he made his way toward the group, he saw that Ashley and Scott were making sneak attacks on their friends. They'd spot somebody, split up, and then slam them from opposite sides.

Michael continued moving toward where all the students were clustered.

After dousing one of their friends, Scott and Ashley were out of water balloons. They ran over to another tub so they could reload.

"All right, that's enough with the water balloons," Mr. Wright said. He was the band director. The chaos was right outside his door.

Students threw their last balloons.

Michael was about fifteen feet behind where all the students were gathered. He was about ten feet from Ashley and Scott.

Michael eyed his water balloon.

"Ashley!" he yelled.

As she turned around, he pelted her right in the face.

MY WAR

What the hell's the matter with you, Michael?" Scott screamed. He ran and pushed Michael.

"Everybody was throwing them," Michael said matter-of-factly.

"It was over, idiot." Scott pushed Michael again. "And besides, you didn't have to throw it at her face!"

Ashley, a large red mark around her eye and forehead, ran over and got between them. She faced Scott, not Michael.

She won't even look at me, he thought. *It's like I don't exist.*

"Just leave him alone, Scott. I told you how he is," Ashley pleaded.

Scott looked at her. Other people were standing around now.

"You're so lucky, dude," Scott stated. He put his finger in Michael's face. "I'd have messed you up."

Then Scott turned to Ashley. He put his arm around her and escorted her away.

Like the prince taking his princess back the castle, Michael thought. *What did she tell him about me? That I'm weird? That I'm a freak?*

As Michael turned to walk away, he saw Mr. Wright.

"I think you'd better go see Principal Licea." Mr. Wright's tone was flat.

Michael knew there was no arguing.

Everybody's against me now.

NO AUTHORITY

And then she wouldn't talk to me after that." Michael hoped he didn't sound frantic as he explained what had happened between him and Ashley. He knew the principal was busy. He didn't have time to listen to all the students' problems.

Principal Licea stared at him from behind his large desk. On it was a computer and a bunch of paperwork. Behind the desk was a bookshelf. The walls were lined with degrees and awards.

"And you thought throwing a water balloon in her face would get her to talk to you again?" Principal Licea's tone was harsh.

He's already against me, Michael thought. *He's already made up his mind.*

"No." Michael was doing his best to remain calm. He knew his breathing was really heavy.

"I'm sorry, Michael. The punishment stands. A week of detention. That'll give you some time to think about all of this."

"This is all I think about anyway!" he cried. "Besides, everybody was throwing water balloons. How come I'm the only one getting in trouble?"

"The other students didn't act maliciously, Michael. You're upset at Ashley, and you deliberately tried to hurt her. You need to stay away from her, or you'll have to deal with harsher consequences. Do you understand, Michael?" Principal Licea glared at him.

This is a nightmare, Michael thought. *I was just trying to have fun. And now I'm in trouble.*

"I really care about her, sir," Michael said slowly. "I would never hurt her."

"You may not think you were hurting her, Michael. You did hurt her, though. You could've broken her nose. Done permanent damaged to her eye."

Michael cringed at the thought.

Is this what Ashley thinks? She can't think I would ever do that. Michael felt a powerful coldness creep over him. He couldn't even talk.

"Michael, you're a junior. Next year you'll be a senior. You're gonna graduate from Willmore, and you'll never have to see Ashley again." The principal was saying exactly what Michael feared the most.

"Is there a counselor or somebody I can talk with?" Michael asked.

"I think you *should* talk to somebody about this. You should tell your parents that you want to. I can make a recommendation to them. We really don't have the staff to handle that sort of thing."

The principal's cell phone buzzed.

He's already forgotten about me. He wants me out of his office so he can get back to work.

"Try thinking about something else. You can't control how other people feel." The principal kept eyeing his phone. "I'm sure your teachers have given you an adequate amount of coursework. Are you taking SAT prep courses?"

In all of Michael's life, he'd never felt so alone and misunderstood.

I'm not even close to being over her. I miss her so much.

THERE TO
REMIND ME

"You really need to forget about Ashley," Kevin kept telling Michael. "Dude, you are *way* obsessing."

"There are so many girls you can go for," John offered.

These seemed to be the only words people were saying to Michael nowadays.

He never thought that seeing Ashley every day would be as traumatic as it was. He felt paralyzed whenever he saw her. He couldn't stop thinking about her.

The worst part? He couldn't call Ashley and tell her how he felt.

If I try to talk to her, she'll probably freak out, and I'll get in even more trouble.

As he spent his week in detention, Michael had the first calming thought he'd had in weeks: *I'd rather be dead than keep seeing her every day. Yeah.*

There was something about that idea—being dead—that made him happier.

This will all end. Who cares if I'm graduating next year? I can't stand the thought of having to see Ashley for another day. I can't stand knowing we will never be together again.

Michael was zoning out all the time now as he kept obsessing about Ashley and what could have been. He would go over the details of their relationship again and again in his mind.

The school held detention in one of the classrooms. The students were supposed to write about why they were in detention, what they had learned, how to improve their behavior, etc.

Michael just stared at his blank sheet of paper.

I'm not going to accept this, he reasoned to himself. *I won't do it.*

I'M GOING
DOWN

Michael got up early that morning. He'd showered the night before so he could leave the house and make as little noise as possible. He put on his clothes, grabbed his backpack, and walked down the hall to his father's study.

On the way there he looked at some pictures of his family that were hanging on the wall. Some were from when Michael was really little; others were more recent.

Those were the good times, he thought.

He stared at one picture of his family on a trip to the mountains. His brothers stood next to their mom, making funny faces. Michael's dad was holding him. He had a stern expression on his face, like always.

You have to do this.

He walked into his father's study. He went over to his desk and opened the main drawer.

He needed the key. He took it and went over to the gun case. He unlocked it and opened the glass door. Michael took the first gun he saw. It was a .22 Magnum.

Even though it's small … it's really heavy.

It was in pristine condition. The handle was dark brown. The main body of the gun was jet black. Michael held the gun up and saw that it had four bullets. He thought about opening it up to make sure all the bullets would fire in succession.

Then he realized he didn't know how to do that. He also realized it didn't matter.

I just need one bullet. Stop wasting time.

Michael put the gun in his backpack and left the house.

HIGHWAY
TO HELL

Walking to school that morning was difficult.

I want to run. I'm used to running.
Normally he only had a few books in his backpack. Michael would tighten up the straps against his back so it didn't bother him.

I can't run with a gun in my backpack.

He passed Otis Park. He stared at the sad playground. Then he looked at the brown grass and the ugly basketball court.

That same feeling he'd had when his

brothers ditched him at the park returned. That one incident cast a long shadow in Michael's life.

I should have just stayed here. I should've gotten more lost and never gone home.

Michael stopped looking at the park even though he wasn't halfway past it.

VANISHING
POINT

Michael spotted Ashley in the quad right away. He'd been watching her for so long, he knew where she'd be at almost any time.

She was with Robin and Hana. They were making a poster.

It's probably for a stupid club, Michael told himself as he walked over to them.

He walked faster than he realized. In seconds he was only a few feet from her.

Ashley didn't look up. She continued to color in the letters on the poster.

Michael saw that the poster was for the Agape Club. He watched Ashley for a moment.

She still doesn't know I'm here. I'm nothing to her now.

Michael slung his backpack around and unzipped it. Still looking at Ashley, he took out the gun.

The more I hold it, the heavier it gets.

Michael held the cold metal at his side.

"I'm sorry, Ashley," he said.

Ashley didn't look up. She just continued coloring in the letters and talking with her friends.

She'll never notice me again. A cold feeling inside Michael was starting to take over.

If he didn't do what he wanted to do, he wasn't going to do it.

I won't give her the chance.

Hana looked up and saw Michael holding the gun. It was still at his side.

"Oh my God!" Hana screamed. "Ashley!"

Ashley looked up and made eye contact with Michael. This was the first time they had looked each other in the eye in a long time.

Since I hurt her with the water balloon.

The gun was still at Michael's side. The cold feeling was increasing. Michael started to raise the gun.

"I love you, Ashley. I love you so much. I'm sorry."

Tears started to come down Michael's cheeks. He hadn't expected to start crying, but he didn't feel like he had any control.

Ashley, Hana, and Robin started to move away from Michael.

Michael was trembling.

"You need to realize what you've done to me," he said.

Suddenly, a large hand grabbed his arm, pulling it down and back. Michael felt another hand forcing him to release the gun.

Then he was thrown to the ground. His face was pressed against the cold concrete.

He felt nothing. Empty. His arms were behind his back. Somebody was sitting on his legs.

"DO NOT MOVE! YOU ARE UNDER ARREST!" a voice said.

"I wasn't going to hurt anyone!" Michael screamed.

He couldn't move at all. Michael started to hyperventilate. He was held so tightly to the ground that he was struggling for air.

Then he heard police sirens.

He saw footsteps of students running as security and more police cleared the campus.

Michael felt handcuffs being put on his wrists. Then he heard a stern voice reading him his rights.

It sounds like Ashley's dad. He started to laugh.

Nobody said anything.

Some hands grabbed him and yanked him to his feet.

He looked around a bit. Aside from campus security and police officers, the quad was empty.

The police officers forcefully walked Michael to the front of the school. There were a lot of police vehicles with swirling red and blue lights.

These are all for me? Why are there so many?

"I wasn't going to hurt anyone," he screamed.

Nobody acknowledged him.

Eventually, Michael was walked to a squad car and put inside. Through the window, he looked around for Ashley, but he didn't see her.

He was done at Willmore.

PRISON-BOUND

From the high school, Michael was taken to the Willmore County Jail.

The first thing they did was give him a medical assessment. Guards took Michael into a cold room and took his handcuffs off. Shortly thereafter, a doctor came in and looked him over.

"Are you in any pain?" he asked as he made some notes on a chart.

"No." Michael's tone was flat and low.

When the doctor left, Michael was taken to another room where there were a few other inmates—is that what he was?—who each had a guard. Some of them looked like they had been in jail before. Others looked how Michael felt. Scared.

He was led over to an area where he had his photo taken. Then Michael was taken to a computer. He put his hand on a machine that looked like a scanner. Images of Michael's fingerprints soon appeared on the screen.

After that, Michael was given a towel and a bar of soap. He was directed to an area where some other people were taking a shower. Guards were watching them the whole time.

NEW
CLOTHES

The person who issued him his blue jump-suit didn't make eye contact. Michael was also given a white shirt, underwear, and black shoes with Velcro closures. The last thing Michael was issued was a toothbrush.

It looks like a lollipop—a stick with a piece of Styrofoam at the end, he thought.

Everyone took their stuff without asking any questions. Michael did the same. They changed into their clothes.

"Man, these things are nasty!" one of

the prisoners stated. Some of his friends laughed.

"My pants are too tight," another one said.

"They better get me some newer kicks." A prisoner held up their issued shoes. "These things are sorry."

Why am I here? Who am I in here with? I didn't do anything. How long will I be here? What does Ashley think? I didn't hurt anybody. How long can they hold me?

A guard then led him and the rest of the new inmates through the facility. There was another guard following. They didn't have guns, but other guards standing around watching them did.

"Straight line," the guard behind them barked.

His voice scared Michael. He knew they wanted him to be scared.

EVERYBODY'S TALKING

The group was led to a room with chairs lined against a wall. Opposite the chairs was an office door. The nameplate read Mr. Boyce.

Michael waited outside with some of the other inmates for a few minutes. Nobody was talking.

They're probably too scared. Michael eyed an inmate who was staring at some other prisoners. He had fierce eyes. *Like if you said the wrong thing, he would pound you into the ground.*

Eventually, it was Michael's turn to go into Mr. Boyce's office. It looked a lot like Principal Licea's. There was a desk, a computer, a stack of files, and a bunch of awards and citations with Mr. Boyce's name on them.

Mr. Boyce shook Michael's hand. Then he told him that he was going to be asking a lot of questions.

"This is part of your intake. I need to get a profile on you," Mr. Boyce commented. He made notes in a file that had Michael's name on it. "You'll be here doing your intake for a few days. You'll probably see the judge. After that, we'll send you over to general housing in Grover. If you don't get to see the judge, we'll take you to Grover and then bring you back here."

"Okay." Michael was finding it really hard to talk now.

"Let's see ... you brought a weapon to school. Is that correct?" Mr. Boyce's tone was indifferent; he was used to asking these kinds of questions.

"I brought my dad's gun. But I didn't bring it as a weapon … " Michael was hoping he was going to let him explain his situation more.

"Why did you target that girl?"

"Ashley?" Michael was surprised by the directness of the question. "I wasn't …

"I see." Mr. Boyce interrupted. And the questions continued.

"Do you have a lot of friends? Do you like being around other people? Are you able to let things go?"

He never asks me to expand on these questions. He doesn't ask for any more information about them. He just asks more questions about different things, Michael thought with mounting irritation. *And he never mentions Ashley by name. He just calls her "that girl" or "the subject" or something like that.*

After what seemed like hours of this, Michael was led over to a glass cell. There was nobody else inside.

NEED

The next day Michael was taken from his cell at the jail and loaded on a bus with a bunch of other inmates. It was the weekend, and he wasn't going to get to see the judge until early the following week. Michael was going to general housing.

I didn't sleep at all last night. He looked around at some of the inmates who were on the bus. There were six of them. Some were staring straight ahead. Others were nodding off. *Is this normal for them? Everybody seems more relaxed than me. I think everybody's looking at me. I think they're just waiting for me to screw up …*

what's gonna happen then?

"That was stupid," one of the inmates said to another. At least that's what Michael thought was said. He didn't want to be caught looking at anybody for too long.

"Who you calling stupid?" somebody snapped back loudly.

"You, punk!"

Michael felt like these two people were on top of him as they argued. He closed his eyes. Even though they were all locked into their seats, Michael didn't like it when people got too loud.

"You boys shut up back there, or I'm gonna come back and shut you up!" the guard at the front of the bus yelled. His voice was loud and stern. The two guys who were arguing stopped.

After a thirty minute ride, the bus pulled up to a large field with a tall wire fence around it. There was a sign out front that read: Grover Youth Detention Facility

The City of Grover was about thirty minutes away from Porterville.

It's even farther from Willmore. Even further from Ashley ...

In the middle of the detention facility were three white buildings. They all looked the same. Armed guards were stationed in different areas near the gate. There were also guards out patrolling the grounds.

"Minors out!" the guard with the shotgun yelled as he stepped on the bus.

Minors? Michael thought. *That's how they refer to us?*

Everybody stood up.

I should be more tired, Michael told himself. *How long can you stay up before your body makes you go to sleep? Maybe that's what everybody's waiting for. They'll get me when I'm sleeping.*

Michael started thinking back to stories he had heard about juvenile hall.

Michael and his friends didn't know anything about this place. They'd heard only rumors.

As he walked across the hard gravel road, he stared at the white nondescript buildings. They had large glass windows, but they were heavily tinted so you couldn't see inside.

All I wanted was to be close to Ashley. Michael found it comforting to think about her. He would be around boys for a long time from what he could tell. *And now? I'm further away from her than ever before.*

WORLDS

The living quarters looked more like a rec room. Inside the building were twenty rooms. Each room had a bed and a small desk. In the common area was a ping pong table and a bunch of white tables with chairs. The minors—provided they followed the rules—could play ping pong and board games and watch TV.

Outside there was a basketball court. Inmates could also run around the field as long as they didn't get too close to the fence.

Michael was told that until he'd been there for a while and proved he could handle himself, he wasn't going to be able to run around the field.

There were guards everywhere. There were also people who worked with the minors. Some were teachers, some were counselors, some were volunteers.

Michael was assigned a bed. He was glad to be alone for a while.

I don't want to look at anybody. I don't want to talk to anybody. I don't belong here. Not with these people.

On the bus he'd listened to chatter about stealing cars, fighting, robbing. He did his best to tune it out.

Just focus on getting released, Michael told himself. *You're going to get out of here. I'm not gonna be here for fourteen months like the lawyer I talked to said I might. When I have my detention hearing, the judge will see that I don't belong in this place. I'm not a felon. I didn't even do anything.*

Michael kept thinking these thoughts as he lay down on his bed. His brain was whirring, but his body was exhausted. Eventually, he fell asleep.

IN *THE* SYSTEM

Every day the minors got up at six o'clock.

That's the same time I used to get up at home, Michael thought as he headed to the showers. *You can sleep in until seven, but then you'll get to the food last, and it's usually not as warm. You also always have to walk around with your hands behind your back.*

Michael was doing his best to remember that: hands behind your back. It was hard.

Grouped by age, inmates were marched out of the housing facility after breakfast. They were led into the teaching facility. Single file. Hands behind their backs.

There's always a guard in the front and a guard in the back. Michael stared straight ahead as he walked with the other minors. *And they always have their guns.*

He looked around. And he realized that he'd been there almost a week. He hadn't even thought about running. He hadn't thought about his teammates.

I love running. I'd probably feel better if I ran. More comfortable. I don't want to get too comfortable here, though.

He had a meeting with the judge after the weekend. It had already been postponed once.

The judge is too busy, Michael was told. *When I see the judge, I hope he can focus on my case now that he's not as backlogged.*

SCHOOL DAZE

They say this is my school ... but it's not my school. Michael was daydreaming as he worked on his Algebra 2 packet. *There's no teacher teaching the class. They just give us packets to do so that when we get out—if we're still in school—we'll be caught up.*

The minors had no homework. There was a sign posted next to the door of the classroom.

NO COURSEWORK IS TO

LEAVE THIS ROOM

The room had two whiteboards, a couple of bookshelves, and a bunch of tables and chairs.

There were two teachers, but they just monitored the students.

They only help you if you ask for it.

Michael could tell he had the hardest work in the class. There were about twelve students.

The only person close to my level in math is doing geometry.

This really bugged him. It was another sign that he didn't belong here.

We're only together because we're close in age.

The students were allowed to work together.

They get one chance, and if they goof off, they're separated. Michael watched as someone argued with the teacher.

"I wasn't doing nothing!" he yelled at the teacher. He was tall and muscular.

"Listen, Alex," the teacher stated sternly. "You either go to another spot and work, or you go back housing."

Inmates didn't want to go back to housing, but that was the only time they got to take work back. They were placed in a small room by themselves. They couldn't leave until the people who ran housing checked their work.

"I'll go to another spot," the inmate glared at the person he was sitting next to. "You better watch it." Then he picked up his packet and sat down at another desk.

Ever since the incident at Willmore, Michael found he was working slower.

I just can't think like I used to. I'm told these classes matter. This place is set up with six classes. That's the only thing that feels like my old life. I'm told when I get out, I'll still be able to finish up my senior year. Everybody just tells me things now.

SENTENCE

Seeing the judge wasn't anything like what Michael thought it would be.

He met his parents, Judge Barajas, and his public defender in the judge's chambers. Again, the judge's chambers reminded Michael of Principal Licea's office.

They all have a lot of books and awards. I'm gonna have awards someday too, if I can.

Nobody really talked to Michael.

The judge and the public defender talked about Michael's case while his parents sat there listening. His mom kept staring at him. Every so often, she patted

Michael on the back. His father looked grim, although he'd nodded his head when the bailiff brought Michael in.

He's probably ashamed of me now. His stomach tightened at the thought. *I want to apologize. I want to explain what happened. I just can't right now.*

After the judge and public defender spoke, the judge eyed some documents in Michael's case.

"Michael, I am going to be sentencing you to the Grover Youth Detention Facility for a period of not less than fourteen months." The judge stopped talking.

I'm going away for fourteen months. Michael was in shock. *That's forever!*

The judge continued talking. He mentioned that he was only being lenient because this was Michael's first offense. When he was released in fourteen months, he wouldn't be able to stay in his parents' home until he was eighteen. He also talked about the severity of Michael's crime—bringing a gun to school. Zero tolerance.

"Do you understand what I have just told you?" the judge asked.

"Yes, sir." Michael's voice was trembling. He was scared, but he didn't have the cold feeling that he was used to. He didn't feel anything.

"Michael, you're just sixteen years old. When you are released, you'll be seventeen. I want you to know that if you'd been over eighteen and committed the same infraction, your sentence would have been a lot longer," the judge lectured. "Use these next fourteen months wisely, young man. Decide if you ever want to be in this much trouble again. Because you'll be in a place much worse than where you are right now." The judge was glaring at Michael.

I'm a criminal, Michael told himself. *I'm a bad guy ... but I'm not.*

MIND GAMES

A few days later Michael met with the psychologist at the Grover Youth Detention Facility. Her name was Laura Sewell.

The first thing Michael noticed was that her office was different than all the others he had been in.

Her office is just a table and two plastic chairs. A few books. It's pretty empty.

As Michael sat down, he noticed that everything on the walls seemed to have been things made for her by the minor inmates. They were mainly drawings, but there were also posters with positive sayings on them.

She's a shrink. She just wants to figure me out or something. He immediately crossed his arms as the session started. *No way am I being analyzed.*

"Tell me about Ashley." Laura smiled warmly.

Michael was surprised at her directness. They had only been talking for a few minutes.

"I'm in love with her," he replied.

"Have you ever been in love before?"

"No … I don't think so. Not like this anyway."

"How did you feel when you were with her?"

"I don't know …"

Laura stared at him. She had a notepad in her hand. She didn't write on it a lot. She seemed to be actually listening to him.

"Connected."

"That's a very good way to describe your feelings." Laura smiled.

"I guess that's what it's like to be in love." Michael looked away after he said that. He started to feel himself getting sad. He was mostly numb now. He didn't think he could afford to be sad anymore.

"Do your feelings scare you?"

"Scare me?"

"Being that connected to somebody. Needing them."

Michael looked down. He knew he'd be asked about Ashley, but he didn't think the questions would be so personal.

"No ... " he started. "I'm more scared about never feeling that way again. Of never getting to see Ashley. Or worse ... what if she hates me?"

Laura would make a few notes when Michael was talking. As soon as he stopped, she stopped writing. Michael liked how she looked at him. How she seemed to take in what he was saying.

Like she's really listening to me.

SEVEN
MONTHS LATER

As much as he didn't want to get comfort-able, Michael had settled into a routine at Grover.

He got up at five thirty a.m. He tried to go to the bathroom and shower before any of the other inmates were up.

I need to be as quiet as possible, he told himself. He no longer needed to remind himself to keep his hands behind his back. He did it automatically.

He also noticed that there were some really tough inmates in general housing.

Those guys are just mean and mad at the world. He didn't want to cross them.

So far, Michael Ellis was doing a good job of keeping to himself.

After breakfast he'd go to school. When he was done, since he didn't have homework, he'd run around the perimeter of the field—without going too near the fence. The authorities let him start running around the three-month mark.

They tell me I'm doing good. I need to stay in shape if I want to rejoin the track team when I leave Grover. Michael didn't know where he was going to go to school after this. But he wanted to be a part of something again. Run for a track team. Anything.

Michael liked running because it got him away from the other minors. Even though he felt caged in at Grover, when he ran, he still felt free.

And that feels good.

After the run, Michael went back to his room and checked to see if he had any mail.

The only people who write me a lot are my mom and brothers. John has written me a few times. Sometimes, before I go into my room, I think I might find a letter from Ashley, but she hasn't sent me one yet.

He rarely got any telephone calls. The only person who called was his mom, but he was never allowed to stay on the phone long. He didn't expect his friends to call. Michael spent his free time reading or watching movies. After that, he'd eat and go to bed.

I do the same thing every day. I don't know how people with really long sentences do it.

One day Michael was running around Grover's field. Two inmates were hanging out nearby. Then they started arguing.

Suddenly, some more inmates ran over.

"What is this?!" screamed one of them.

Then everybody started to beat up a particular inmate. They punched him and kicked him to the ground, where they continued to pummel him.

Michael watched this for a moment and then looked away. He heard guards yelling as they ran over. Michael hated seeing violence like this. He hated seeing people being hurt.

I wish I could've helped that person, he thought. *I wish I could've stopped those guys. I'm too scared to do anything. I don't want to get beaten up.*

TEN MONTHS
LATER

You say you weren't going to hurt Ashley?" Laura asked.

Michael glared at her. He suddenly felt bathed in the cold feeling that he always got anytime he thought about Ashley and the bad time at Willmore.

"I wasn't." He was trying to talk in short sentences. He figured the less he said, the quicker the subject would be changed.

I don't mind talking about Ashley, Michael thought. *Or about what happened with her ... but I don't want to talk about that day. That didn't have anything to do with us.*

"You had a gun. Did you want to scare her?"

"I didn't want to scare anybody." Michael caught himself. He had raised his voice. Laura didn't seem fazed at all.

She probably has people yell at her all the time.

"I wanted to make a statement."

"With a gun?" Laura's expression was unchanged. There was something about her questions. Michael didn't feel like she was trying to trick him. She just wanted to understand him better. That was why Michael wasn't getting too angry. He knew Laura cared about him, and it made him feel better.

"The only person I hurt was myself." Michael was really trying not to get emotional. To not think of everything he'd lost by doing what he did.

"Were you suicidal?"

Michael pursed his lips slightly. He took a deep breath.

"Would you like some water?" Laura asked.

"No," Michael started, "I shouldn't have brought the gun to school. It's just … nobody would listen to me. I tried to talk to people. Nobody wanted me to talk about Ashley or what I was going through."

Laura stared at him.

"Thank you for talking to me," he said finally.

TWELVE
MONTHS LATER

I've been in here a year, but I don't feel any different.

Michael was running around the field.

It was a cold December afternoon. The sky was gray. Michael liked running when it was cold. It reminded him of the cold nights when he and Ashley first started hanging out.

He looked at the inmates as he ran around the perimeter of the field for the third time that day.

I thought guys would mess with me. The thing is, of the guys who got here the same day I did, I'm the only one still here. Maybe since I didn't make an effort to meet anybody, the other inmates figured I must be crazy or something. Maybe that's why they left me alone.

He talked to people in his classes or in the common area, but they weren't friends.

I don't ask them a lot of questions like I would John or Kevin or someone from Willmore. The people here only talk to me if they need help with their schoolwork.

Michael's mom was going to be visiting later in the week. She came a couple times a month. His dad hadn't come once. He hadn't seen his father since that day in the judge's chambers.

She always says he's going to come, but then he doesn't, and she makes an excuse for him.

The days blended together. They moved along like any twenty-four hours. Only Michael's life was anything but normal.

Two months to go, but he wasn't going home. Until Michael turned eighteen, he'd be staying with his grandmother in Adlerville.

Forty miles from Willmore. Savage Continuation School, I wonder what that's like. That should look great on my transcripts.

Michael continued running.

Maybe when I get out, if I'm really lucky, things'll be different for me. I want them to be. I want to be okay. Feel okay. But I'm scared I won't ever be okay again. But I want to be.

RAIN ON ME

Michael walked down the same gravel road that he had come in on. He stared at the fence that he'd run around every day. He watched as some of the inmates played basketball or talked on the field.

He hadn't made a single friend the whole time he'd been at Grover. The only thing Michael had done was stay up on his schoolwork. And he'd stayed in running shape.

I want to just pick up where I left off before all of this happened, he thought. *I've gotta get my diploma now.*

Michael turned his attention to the

road ahead and saw his mom and Erik waiting for him. They were standing by Erik's car.

"Your father would've come, but he had to work," his mom said. She gave him a hug. Erik did too.

"You look good, Michael," Erik said. Michael knew he was skinnier. He hadn't eaten like he ate at home.

As Michael got in the car, he took one last look at the facility that had been his home for the past fourteen months.

I don't have any connection to this place. And after being away so long, I feel less connected to the people in my family.

Nobody said much during the drive.

It's probably because I'm not going to Porterville.

Michael looked at the old suitcase sitting next to him on the seat. He figured it was filled with his clothes.

That suitcase is probably something

my dad's had forever. He never throws anything away. He's probably mad that he has to lend it to me.

Michael's mom and his brother started talking. He tuned them out and stared out the window.

They drove through Willmore and kept going. Michael was going to his grandmother's in Adlerville. It was a drive. Forty minutes past Willmore.

In a couple of weeks, Michael would be attending Savage Continuation School. A school for misfits.

As the car moved down the freeway, Michael ignored the cold feeling and the tightness in his stomach as he was taken to another place that wasn't home.

At least I'll be able to go home on some of the weekends, he thought.

He closed his eyes for a moment. Then he opened them. He thought he felt some tears coming on. He hadn't cried in fourteen months. And he wasn't going to start now.

He took out his cell phone that his mom had given back to him. She was paying for it. Michael figured that his dad didn't know.

He wouldn't want to pay for something like that for me now. His loser son.

Michael tried to turn on the phone, but it was dead. *Don't get upset. Everything's going to be okay,* he told himself.

Michael Ellis didn't want to believe that, he *had* to believe it.

ON PAROLE

Michael Bryan Ellis." His name rolled off the lips of his parole officer. His name was Allen. He had slick black hair and wore a tan leather jacket. He was reading through Michael's file.

Allen had a tiny office. It was crammed with files. He only displayed two pictures. Michael assumed that the people in them were his wife and child. He had a few books on a shelf. His office didn't have a window.

"How'd you like Grover?" Allen didn't look up from the file.

"I didn't deserve to be there." It

bothered Michael that Allen didn't look at him. "The people there had done really bad things. I'm not like that."

"How do you know that?" Allen glanced at Michael, and then went back to looking at his file.

"I'm not like that," Michael stated firmly, raising his voice.

Calm down, he pleaded to himself. *Stay cool. You just got out. Don't give them a reason to put you away and forget about you again.*

"I didn't hurt anybody." Michael's tone was lower, and he tried to talk slower. "I was the one who was hurt. I still am."

Allen closed the file and put it on his desk. Then he stared directly into Michael's eyes.

"You say you weren't going to hurt anyone, but you brought a loaded gun to school. What were you going to do?" Allen's tone was indifferent.

Tell him! Michael told himself. *Tell him you weren't going to hurt anybody. Just tell him the truth.*

Michael felt himself starting to get that cold feeling. He was used to it by now, but the familiarity seemed to only make it worse. He took slow, deliberate breaths. He didn't say anything.

"I heard from the people at Grover that you were a model ward." Allen leaned back in his chair. "But I'm telling you, Michael Bryan Ellis, if you don't allow yourself to get past this—all the progress you've made—it will be for nothing. As if it were never done."

Allen stood up and opened the door to the office. "You ready?"

Michael nodded his head. He knew what was coming. Random drug tests.

He can come to my house any time and do this. That thought stayed in Michael's head as Allen followed him into the bathroom. It was across the hall from his office.

Allen stood next to him by the urinal. He handed Michael a cup that had a twist cap on it. He watched as Michael unzipped his pants and urinated into it.

He handed the cup to Allen when he was done. Michael didn't look at him the whole time.

ONE WEEK LATER

Michael was walking to Savage Continuation School. It was about a mile from his grandma's house. He eyed his schedule as he went.

He had four classes: geometry, English, social studies, and biology. His classes began at seven thirty. He was done at twelve thirty. The plan was to complete these courses and graduate on time. These particular classes would prepare him for his exit exam.

I want to take the SATs. His mom had

bought him a book to help him study. *The problem is that every time I start to read the book, I get confused.*

Michael's brain fog continued. In fact, his confusion had only increased since he'd gotten out of Grover. He felt numb and listless.

Besides, I'm in a continuation school now. There's no student activities, no dances, no track team. Nothing.

Michael looked up Savage Continuation on Google Earth using his grandma's computer. The grounds had a large grass field with some bleachers for students to socialize on.

Maybe they'll let me run around it?

That thought really depressed him.

The best thing I have to look forward to is maybe I can run around the school field?

He hated that he couldn't live with his parents until he was eighteen. He also hated that he was going to have to take the bus to see them.

The bus from Adlerville to Porterville takes forever. He'd looked it up online. *Ugh. It's like a two hour bus ride because there are so many stops on the way.*

He wished his parents could pick him up, but his mom didn't drive on the freeway.

"I don't like being on the road with all those other cars," she'd told him. "It scares me."

His dad was always working.

He says he can't come and get me. But I think he just doesn't want to.

Michael told himself to knock it off. Stop the negative thinking. It was just making him more upset.

You need to give yourself a chance to be successful.

He was already tired because he had trouble sleeping the night before. He was nervous about his new school.

I hope they're not as stuck-up as the kids at Willmore. That they'll listen to me when I talk.

Michael tried to tell himself that it would be that way.

SAVAGE CONTINUATION

The first thing Michael noticed when he got on the Savage campus was that it was a lot smaller than Willmore. It had three medium-sized red brick buildings with a quad in the middle. There were four tables and a few benches where students could sit. There was also a separate cafeteria that was a little smaller than the three main buildings. Behind all of this was the field that Michael had seen online.

Michael's first stop was to the office

of Mrs. Sefer. She was his guidance counselor. She was a small woman with short red hair.

She's going to be checking my bag every morning, Michael thought as he handed it to her.

He had been told about this search the week before. Michael and his parents had attended a meeting at the Adlerville School District. Savage's principal, Mrs. Sefer, his teachers, and some other members of the school staff were there.

"You excited about your first day?" Mrs. Sefer asked in a peppy voice as she looked through all the compartments of his bag.

"Yeah, I guess."

"You guess? Come on, Michael. You've got to be more excited than that." Mrs. Sefer smiled. "You're gonna be a high school graduate soon."

Michael liked her. She reminded him

of Laura Sewell, the psychologist from Grover.

She's way nicer than my parole officer.

As Michael walked to class, he passed a bunch of students. Michael noticed some of them were girls. One of them even had the same long brown hairstyle as Ashley.

Maybe I'll make friends here. Maybe I'll meet another girl.

Michael's thoughts immediately turned to something else. He couldn't think about that yet.

SCRATCH THE SURFACE

Michael had had so many things on his mind that he forgot his snack money.

I'm glad I'm only here for five hours, he thought as he left school for the day. *I'm starving. I'll just eat a big lunch at my grandma's.*

Michael knew continuation school in Adlerville was going to be different, but he didn't expect it to be almost exactly like Grover.

The teachers don't really teach here either. That bothered him. *There's one in each room, along with some aides. We all work out of our own packets. I thought I was getting out of jail, but it's like I'm still there.*

Michael hadn't had a chance to ask anybody about running on the track.

It doesn't matter anyway.

"How'd it go?" Michael's grandma asked as he walked in the door.

"It was good," he said.

He didn't know what else to say.

"You have a lot of homework?"

"No, they don't really give us homework. We do it all at the school."

"Oh."

Michael could tell by his grandma's response that she thought this whole thing was weird. She didn't understand why Michael did what he did.

She's scared of me now.

Michael walked past her and went into his room.

My whole family is scared of me. They barely talk to me. It's like they think I might attack them or something.

Michael lay down on the small bed in the room his grandma was letting him use. The only other things in there were a desk, a dresser, and a closet. He didn't bring a lot of things from his parents' house. Like Grover, he didn't want to get too comfortable.

I've let everybody down. I wanted to be a doctor—to work with kids. Now I can barely think straight. He took a deep breath and exhaled slowly. *Whatever happens to me from now on, I'm in charge of making my life better.*

Michael heard the front door to his grandma's house open. It must be his cousin Dave. He also lived there.

He's lived with her for a while, I guess. He delivers packages for work, and he helps Grandma out because she's kind of old now. He's big and strong; probably got that way from his job.

Michael decided he was gonna ask his grandma if he could help out around the house. He didn't want to be there and not contribute anything.

LOOKING
GLASS SELF

A few nights later Michael was sitting in his room. He was trying to read his SAT prep book.

I can't follow this. After the introduction about what the book was and wasn't, it described the kinds of questions that would most likely be on the test. Then it started describing how to answer those questions.

I'm lost. I don't get it. I can't focus.

Michael stared at the book. He realized he was thinking about Ashley again.

He thought about the good times. He had trained his mind to avoid thinking about the bad times. And he never thought about that day at school with the gun. Grover only came into his mind when something reminded him of it. Savage was too new for him to have any memories yet.

His cell phone rang.

It was John. Michael hadn't had a call from him on his cell phone in a long time. At first Michael was hesitant about answering it. Then he realized this was his only real link to Willmore. To Ashley.

"How's school? How do you like Adlerville?" John asked.

"It's okay. I wish I was at Willmore." Michael didn't want to talk about where he was living now.

"How are your classes? You made any friends?"

John's questions kept coming.

It's like he just wants me to accept my

new life. Adlerville isn't my home! I love my grandma, but it's not like living with my family. Michael hadn't expected that John's phone call would make him feel so bad.

"How's Ashley?" Michael finally asked.

John was silent.

"Hello?"

"She's cool, I guess." John sounded like he was really trying to say the right thing.

He's afraid I might get upset if he tells me the wrong thing. People probably told him not to talk about her with me. Michael was tired of people walking on eggshells around him. He didn't want them to be mean. He didn't want them to ignore his feelings either. *I just want to be treated like I'm normal.*

"I don't really talk to her," John went on. "I never did."

If Michael thought he was far away from Ashley before he answered his phone, he felt a lot further now.

HARD TIMES

Michael was sitting alone at snack time.

A few days before, he'd had a meeting with Mrs. Sefer. She told him that after talking with his parents, the best thing right now would be for Michael to focus on taking his exit exam and graduating. This way he could graduate with his class year, go to a community college, and then to a university.

Great way to get started as a doctor. Not.

Lately it seemed like Michael got out of bed and was smacked with a dose of bad news.

The worst part was he kept thinking about Ashley's dad.

He'd probably be so happy to know about this. He never thought I was anything. This just proves it.

Michael stared at his half-eaten apple. He also had an unopened orange juice.

Everyone has moved on from what happened—everyone but me.

Michael got up and went for a walk around campus. He didn't know what he was hoping to accomplish, but he wasn't getting anywhere staring at his food.

This place is so ugly, he thought. *It looks how I feel.*

"How's it going, Michael?" He turned around and saw Mrs. Sefer standing behind him.

She's probably here to tell me something else that's gone wrong for me.

"Okay."

"Something on your mind?" The

guidance counselor genuinely seemed like she wanted to know.

"To be honest, I miss my old school."

"That's understandable." Mrs. Sefer smiled. "You just started here."

"Yeah." Michael looked at the ground.

Everybody always has quick and easy answers for my situation. I totally derailed my life. Why is everybody acting like I can just get back on track so easily? he wondered.

"Give this place a chance," Mrs. Sefer continued. "You owe it to yourself to get a fresh start."

"What if I don't want to start fresh somewhere else? What if I was fine where I was."

"Then you wouldn't be here, right?" Mrs. Sefer's tone was a little sterner but still friendly.

"There isn't anything fun here. I was on the track team at my old school. I had friends. I don't have anything here. This school doesn't have anything for me. I'm just studying to prepare me for the exit exam. Why don't I just test out right now and get it over with?"

"I understand where you're coming from." Mrs. Sefer's voice was calm and even. "But like I said, give it a little more time. You have a lot of people who are rooting for you, and that will help you, Michael. You can still do everything you want to do. You just have to adjust your plans a bit."

They spoke for a little while longer, then Mrs. Sefer had to go.

She's nice, Michael thought as he continued walking around the Savage campus. *I don't mind her checking my bag every morning.*

TIME OUT
OF MIND

Tonight was one of those rare nights when Michael was home alone with his cousin Dave. His grandma was at Bible study with some friends.

Michael made himself a sandwich and was walking through the living room to get to his room.

"Hey."

"Hi," Dave said, never taking his eyes off the TV.

All he does when he's not working is watch TV and play video games. He helps my grandma out but only when she asks.

Michael shut the door to his room and put his sandwich on the table. *I think video games are okay, but after everything I've been through, I'd rather be outside running or something.*

For a split second Michael thought about hanging out with Dave. Then Michael realized every time he'd tried to talk to Dave, he'd just gotten one-word answers.

A run would calm him down, but he didn't feel like it. Ever since he'd gotten out of Grover, he didn't feel like doing much of anything.

COMING
HOME

Michael's mom picked him up at the Porterville bus station on Friday night. He'd
wanted to get out of town right when
he got out of school, but his grandma
worked until five. Dave was working
a swing shift from noon to nine, so he
couldn't take him. Michael left Adlerville
at six thirty.

"Your dad was supposed to come, but
he had to work later than he thought," his
mom told Michael as they drove through
town.

Michael noticed that everything looked the same but different. It was like he was staring at familiar places through fog.

"Dad always has to work," Michael stated.

"Well, he does like to provide for us." His mom stared at the road.

I feel like a burden to everybody, Michael thought as he sat in the front seat. *My mom doesn't even seem happy to have me home. It's like she and my dad have to let me come home, like it's an obligation. They probably can't wait until I'm eighteen. Then they can cut me loose.*

Dinner was even worse. Nobody said anything. You could only hear the sounds of people chewing, silverware clanking, and water or soda being sipped.

My dad won't even look at me. If I'm not a doctor, I'm nothing to him. Michael was staring at his food. Every so often, he stole a glimpse at his father. If they made eye contact, his dad was the first to look away.

What kind of a doctor would I make anyway? I'm so messed up. How could I help people?

Michael told himself to change the subject.

You have to stop this. What's done is done. Nobody cares if you cry. Nobody cares about you.

"Erik and Jason couldn't come this weekend," Michael's mother finally said to break the silent tension.

They were supposed to come and visit Michael on his first weekend home. Michael thought that coming home for the first time would be more of a big deal.

I don't matter to anyone. Nothing matters. I'm just a loser to them.

LIFE. LOVE. REGRET.

Michael couldn't sleep. His chest felt tight. He could breathe but it wasn't effortless.

Michael walked quietly around the house. He didn't want to wake his parents.

Then he found himself in his father's study. It looked almost exactly the same. The only difference was that all of Dad's guns were gone from the glass case. There was even an official note posted there from the police department. Basically, the note read that the guns had been confiscated.

Michael stared at the empty gun case.

It was so quiet in the house he could hear himself breathing.

You need to get out of this room.

He quickly turned off the light in the study, walked back to his bedroom, and stood in the doorway.

Suddenly, he saw his father standing in the hallway. They locked eyes and just stared at each other.

"Good night," his dad said.

Michael noticed that he seemed to smile when he said that. Like he'd smiled when Michael was little.

I'm just imagining it.

"Good night," Michael said.

His dad turned and walked into the bathroom.

"I'm … I'm sorry," Michael stuttered.

As he heard his father lock the bathroom door, he realized he'd said it too quietly. His father hadn't heard him.

NOTHING

The next day Michael went for a walk around Porterville. He tried calling John on his cell phone, but he didn't pick up.

Why do I even have a cell phone? Nobody calls me anyway.

He put the phone back in his pocket.

For a split second he thought about walking into Willmore. He knew he couldn't go to Ashley's house, but what if he ran into her?

What would I say to her? What would she say? Does she think about me?

Michael decided against it. He didn't want Ashley to see him like this. To see him so down.

As he walked, he passed Otis Park.

I wish I could go to the park and come out as a kid again, he thought. *I'd give anything for a do-over. Then I wouldn't be a bother to anybody. My parents, my grandma, the school system, Ashley. Everybody can just be happy, and I won't be in any trouble. God, I hate feeling so pathetic.*

A LIGHT IN THE DARK

Michael was really tired on Monday after his weekend at home.

He had been listless at school, going through the motions. He did the work in his packets. He ate alone at snack time. Then he'd come home and volunteered to do some yard work for his grandma.

Something about my life has got to change, he told himself as he was sweating in the sun, pulling weeds. *This can't be all there is.*

The future. It had really been on Michael's mind a lot.

I really screwed myself. What am I going to do now? I never thought of being anything other than a doctor. Now what?

He knew he could probably still be a doctor, but he didn't think he had the mind for it. He didn't feel mentally capable.

Not anymore.

He hated that he was felon. Michael knew there were some people who would be stoked to be that. They would go out of their way to be hardened.

That's not me at all.

Back in his room, Michael tried to think of other things he could do with his life. Then his phone rang.

It was John.

Finally, I can talk to somebody who knows the old me!

"Hey, bro," John started. "Sorry I wasn't around last weekend when you were here. You didn't leave me a message."

Michael had wondered if maybe John and his other friends were avoiding him now.

Maybe they don't want to know me anymore after what happened.

He told himself to stop thinking so much—to enjoy the conversation with his friend.

"It's cool. I'm hoping to come down twice a month until I graduate."

"What happens after that?" John asked.

"I turn eighteen a week later. I'll be an adult. I can move back to my parents' house then. I'll probably go to community college for a couple years, then transfer somewhere."

"Cool. That's cheaper than starting at a four-year school."

For the first five minutes of the conversation, Michael felt like he was racking his brain, trying to think of things to say.

It was never like this before. I used to be able to talk to people. Now all I do is think about everything, but I don't figure anything out.

"We were thinking," John continued. "Since you're at that new school now, and you're not gonna be able to walk with us at graduation, if the people at Willmore are cool with it … maybe you could go to our prom?"

Michael perked up. He couldn't believe what he was hearing. Was he being given a chance to return to Willmore? To show everybody in his class that despite what had happened, he was still around? To show Ashley and everybody else that there was nothing wrong with him?

"Yeah, I'd like that," he said. "Thanks for thinking about me. When is it?"

"June second. Kevin and I were thinking we could also come down there and pick you up. So you don't have to take the bus."

"You guys would do that for me?" Michael hadn't heard news this good in a while.

"Yeah, we're your friends. We miss you. We want you to be with us."

ALIVE

Michael was so amped up after talking to John that he decided to go for a run. The sun was starting to set, and he wanted to get one in before it was completely dark. He still didn't one hundred percent know his grandma's neighborhood.

I'd hate to get lost and have my grandma or Dave think I was an idiot because they had to come get me.

It was a nice evening for running. There weren't many people out, and Michael ran inside a park so he wasn't around a lot of cars and traffic. The park had a lot of trees, small hills, and greenery.

The cold air, the trees ... it still reminds me of Ashley so much. When things were better.

He started to get that cold feeling again. Remembering when he and Ashley were still getting to know one another. Then he remembered his conversation with John.

You need to start saving your money, setting goals, he told himself. *You'll need a part-time job if you're going to rent a tuxedo.*

As Michael ran, he jumped over a small rock.

This is the start of something. I wanted to take Ashley to that dance, but it all got taken away from me. The Willmore prom is my last chance to make something happen. It's my last chance to reconnect with Ashley so she can remember why she liked me in the first place.

Was this his second chance? Was he finally moving through the trauma of what happened? For just a moment, he wasn't thinking about Ashley or anybody else. He was thinking about himself. And that felt good.

KEEPIN' ON

Later in the week, Michael had to postpone his after school job hunt to visit his parole officer.

God, I hate having to report to him. It wastes so much time taking the bus to see him. By the time I get done and get home, the day is over.

As Michael stewed, Allen sat across from him going through his paperwork. His desk seemed to have three times as many files on it than when Michael first saw him.

Allen made him pee in a cup at start of their meeting. It was exactly the same procedure as it was the first time.

Then he asked Michael a few questions.

"How's school going?"

"How's the new living situation?"

"You think you'll be prepared for your exit exam? Graduate?"

Michael answered all the questions. Then the parole officer's phone rang.

"You're cool. See you in a few weeks," Allen said as he picked it up.

I shouldn't have to come here. I shouldn't have to go to the bathroom in front of him, Michael thought as he stepped into the creaky elevator in the old building.

Allen seemed like he had a lot of work to do today. Maybe he'll get so busy that he'll forget about me. I hope he does. I'll never really feel comfortable until I don't have anything to do with Allen, the courts, the legal system. I just want to be really free.

CARL

Michael had senior projects in English and history. He hadn't picked what his topics were going to be. He should have—he'd had the topic list for over a week. He was supposed to work with a partner for the history project, but he was unmotivated to find one.

For history, I want to write about something that hasn't changed from the past to now. I want to write about injustice.

A new student walked into the class. He wore black shorts and a blue tank top. He had a lot of muscles, like he worked out every day. His brown hair was buzzed short. The new student gave the teacher, Mrs. Simone, a piece of paper.

"Why don't you take a seat near Michael, " she said, indicating an empty chair with a nod of her head. "And I'll find a packet that's at your level."

The student walked over and sat next to Michael. There were three long tables in the classroom all facing the whiteboard. The teacher's desk was off to the side of the room.

"Michael," Mrs. Simone called across her desk. "Do you have a partner for your senior project yet?"

"No, Mrs. Simone."

"Why don't you partner with Carl?"

"Okay."

Michael looked at Carl.

"I'm Michael."

They shook hands.

"Carl."

They sat there in silence.

"Do you have anything you want to do for a history project?" Michael asked.

Carl shrugged.

He just got into the class, you idiot, Michael berated himself. *He probably just wants to be left alone. Same as you.*

"I was thinking about doing something on injustice. We could talk about something from history where somebody was accused of doing something—which they actually did do—but they shouldn't have gotten in trouble for it."

"That'd be cool with me," Carl said.

"Okay. Now we just have to think of something that's like that."

Michael eyed the computer across the room.

"Maybe we could look up something on the Internet?"

"Whatever," Carl sighed.

They got Mrs. Simone's permission and went over to the computer. Michael started searching "historical injustice."

"How long have you been here?" Carl asked as a bunch of links came up on the screen.

"A little over a month," Michael answered.

Carl nodded his head.

"I had some problems at my old school," Michael offered.

"Of course you did. We all did." Carl smiled. "Otherwise we wouldn't be here."

"Yeah." Michael was finding it hard to concentrate on the links and talk at the same time. "The people there … they were really judgmental."

"Screw them," Carl snapped. "It's good you bailed. You shouldn't let anybody push you around, or tell you what to do."

"Or how to feel," Michael added.

At that moment, Rina, a girl in the class, walked past them. She had dark black hair with blonde streaks in it. She always wore tight jeans with tight tucked-in shirts. There was no denying she was pretty hot.

Michael and Carl watched her walk by.

"I think I'm gonna like this school." Carl smiled again.

Michael smiled slightly.

It's so easy for somebody like him, Michael thought. *One girl is just the same as another to him. It's all physical for most guys. But it's not like that for me. When I see a girl like Rina? All that does is make me think about Ashley even more.*

MONEY, MONEY, MONEY

Michael threw the last of the trash away in a can on the side of his grandma's house. His grandma was paying him to do chores now, and so far Michael had made fifty dollars.

I hate taking money from her. I just have to be able to go to prom, but at the rate I'm going, it's not gonna happen. I won't have enough money.

He'd thought about asking his parents for money, but he knew he couldn't.

They wouldn't help me. They don't have any money anyway.

Michael had set a goal of two hundred dollars.

I need at least that if I'm gonna pull off the tux and dinner. I might even need more if I end up paying for Ashley.

That thought made him want to go out and look for a job right then and there. It was almost eight.

"I wish I could pay for John. To thank him for sticking with me and bringing me back to Willmore."

It was the end of April. June second was about five weeks away, and Michael was behind his goal in earning money.

MR. TROUT

Running home from school a few days later, Michael saw that Subway was hiring. He went inside, filled out the application, and turned it in to the person behind the counter.

He hesitated when he got to the box that asked if he had ever been arrested. He checked yes. He wasn't going to lie.

"You want to talk to the manager now?" the employee asked.

Michael hadn't expected to see the manager, but he was glad he could.

"Yes, please. Thank you."

He hoped he didn't sound too desperate.

Before Michael knew what was happening, he was in the office of Mr. Trout, the manager of Subway.

The walls were covered with work schedules, labor law information, and data on store sales. Mr. Trout had a computer on his desk and some pictures of people that Michael figured were his family.

"Everything looks good, Michael," Mr. Trout said, eyeing his application.

Michael had run a paper route for five years; he'd also been a summer camp counselor. He'd wanted to get more work experience at a place like Subway, but being so involved in school—trying to get in as many advanced courses as he could—precluded that.

"I'd like to offer you the job," Mr. Trout said. He smiled. Michael couldn't help smiling back. "When are you available?"

"I can work Monday through Thursday anytime after twelve thirty."

"And how about weekends—what's your availability?"

Michael hadn't thought about how important that might be.

"Sometimes. I live with my grandma. I usually go home and see my parents on the weekends."

Michael wasn't sure if he should've told Mr. Trout that. But he just knew that saying he had to be available for his family was an excuse a lot of people wouldn't argue with.

Mr. Trout flipped the application around.

"You go to Savage ..."

Michael could see the dawning realization in Mr. Trout's expression. He must know Savage was the continuation school. The "problem kid" high school.

He's gonna find out about the felony, he thought nervously. *He's gonna see it on the application.*

Michael started to get cold inside. He could even feel himself starting to shake. His mouth suddenly felt dry. He'd mainly been numb since he left Grover, which was better than how he was feeling now.

Stay calm. Just tell him what you can tell him. Tell him the truth. You need to start being comfortable with who you are for once.

"I had some problems at my old school, and I had to leave," Michael said.

Those thirteen words were probably the hardest ones Michael had ever said.

"So that's why I'm living here."

Mr. Trout continued to eye the application.

"Well, I just need to do a background check and verify your references. Then we'll get you on the schedule and set up a training routine." Mr. Trout smiled.

"I have the job?" Michael was ecstatic.

"I don't see why not."

Mr. Trout extended his hand. Michael shook it.

"Welcome aboard, Michael. I give everyone a chance. And I think you're gonna do great here. So don't disappoint me."

"I won't. And thank you, Mr. Trout. Thank you!"

Michael walked home in a daze.

Mr. Trout had seen his application. He knew about Michael; he knew what he was.

And it was okay.

I'll just keep working on myself. Keep moving forward in my own way. Take my time.

GIRL U WANT

I'm gonna be able to go for sure," Michael told John as he got closer to his grandma's house.

Michael was walking so fast as he talked on the phone that he was practically jogging.

"Awesome! It's gonna be so great to have you back here," John said.

"Have you spoken to Principal Licea yet?" Michael held his breath after he asked.

Those people have the power to stop it, he thought to himself. *I hope they don't. I need to go to this prom. I need to show*

Ashley—I need to show everybody—that I'm not a monster. That I'm okay.

"I think Kevin did. He was stoked to hear that you might be coming," John stated.

"Awesome!" Michael could barely contain himself.

"It's gonna be cool. I might even have a girl for you to go with. Do you remember Api Wiseman?"

Michael paused for a moment. He did remember Api.

She was cool, but I don't really know her. Why would I want to take her to prom? he wondered.

"It's cool. You don't need to ask her." Michael hoped he didn't ungrateful.

"Why not?"

"I wanna go with Ashley."

"Dude, she's probably going with someone."

"Who?"

"I don't know, but she probably is. It's her senior prom. If she's going, I doubt she's gonna go solo."

"Well," Michael started, "if I'm not going with her, I'd rather go alone."

"Uh, okay," John said.

Michael could tell by the way he said it that John didn't understand.

HASHING
IT OUT

Michael and Carl were sitting together during snack.

Michael was eating a granola bar and an apple. Carl was eating a breakfast burrito. He put it down and took a big swig of his orange juice.

"This thing's gross." Carl made a face.

Michael laughed.

"I think that's the first time I've seen you smile."

"Really?" Michael asked.

*I probably don't smile a lot. Or laugh.
I need to work on that.*

Then he told Carl about his plan to go
back Willmore's prom.

"You should go back there. Show them
that you're still around." Carl had a stern
look on his face, like he meant what he
said.

*Like being tough and mean comes easy
to him.*

"I hope the people at my old school
agree with you," he said.

"You have something you want to do?
You need to make it happen. Haven't those
people messed with you enough?"

"Yeah, you're right," Michael agreed.

As mad and upset as he still was about
everything that had happened, Michael
never wanted to be mean or hurt anyone.

I just don't want to be ignored.

ENDLESS
LOVE

Michael sat in English class reading the copy of *Wuthering Heights* that Mrs. Gerlich had given him. He chose to write a report on it for his senior project.

He was only on page five, and he was lost. The way the characters talked, the descriptions, it all confused him. English was not his favorite subject. If only he was with Ashley now. She would walk him through this classic.

The only reason I chose this book is because I read the back cover, he thought.

The main characters, Heathcliff and Cathy, they can't be together for some reason. It's kinda like me and Ashley.

Michael knew that if the old Michael were reading this book, he would have been able to focus. He would have been able to get through it. The words would not blur on the page.

I was so much smarter before everything happened.

He was starting to get depressed. He'd been trying to work on his reading, but the words just swam on the page.

Now I just feel like there are so many barriers in my thought processes. Like I can't get passed myself. I'm in the way. And I don't know what to do.

After reading the same sentence over and over, he stopped. He flipped through the book, realizing he had a long way to go before he was finished.

I'm never going to finish. This report

is due in a little over a month. I wish I had more time. Everything is so go-go-go.

This isn't what I thought my senior year would be. I should be coasting by now. My college acceptance letters should be rolling in.

I WON'T
LET ME

Michael had been working at Subway for a little over a week. So far he was doing pretty well. He was getting better at making the sandwiches. He knew how to work the cash register, and all of his coworkers seemed to like him. Even the customers had been cool for the most part.

He had ten minutes left in his shift. He had been so into what he was doing that he hadn't even noticed Carl walk in. Michael looked up. Carl was standing in front of him.

"Cold cut combo, bro. Twelve-inch," Carl said. He had a smile in his eyes.

Michael suddenly got nervous. Being at Grover had made him a lot more street smart. Carl's smile said a lot.

Michael made him the sandwich.

"You want anything else with that?" Michael asked.

"Large drink."

Michael put the sandwich and an empty soda cup on the counter. He was about to ring it up.

"Can you hook it up, Mike?"

Michael looked at him. He knew this was coming. Carl wanted his order for free. If Michael was normal, not a felon, this wouldn't be a problem.

If he hooked it up, he could get in a lot of trouble.

"It'd violate my parole if I got caught," Michael said in a low tone. He stared at Carl with as hard a look as he could muster.

"It's cool, bro." Carl flashed his usual smile and reached for his wallet.

Michael rang up his order.

If I'm gonna violate my parole, he thought, *it's not gonna be over a sandwich.*

Carl filled his cup and sat down to eat.

"Mike." Carl waved him over a few minutes later. He was about halfway done with his sandwich.

Michael walked over and sat down. He still didn't like when people called him Mike, but he didn't mind it as much with Carl.

He doesn't sound like he's putting me down when he says it.

"Sorry about that before," Carl said. "I didn't know about you being on parole."

"It's okay."

"I got in trouble too. It's why I was

sent from my old high school to Savage."
Carl took a sip of his drink.

Michael felt himself getting uneasy.
He really didn't want to talk about how
he'd gotten in trouble. At the same time,
he was curious about Carl's story.

"Do you miss your old school?"
Michael asked.

"I miss my friends. I miss that I didn't
get to graduate with them. They graduated
last year, and I'm still finishing up."

"Oh." Michael wanted to know why
Carl had to leave his old school. If his
story was anything like his.

"I stole my parents' car. I ended up
crashing it pretty bad. Broke my collar
bone. I had to miss a bunch of school. I
got sent to Savage to get caught up."

"Why'd you steal the car? Was it an
emergency and your parents wouldn't let
you use it?" Michael could imagine himself doing something like that for Ashley.

"Nah." Carl took a big bite of his sandwich. "I just wanted to drive it. It was stupid. What about you? Why're you on parole?"

Michael felt his stomach turn. He thought there'd be more to Carl's story. That Carl had been in desperate situation and had no choice but to steal his parents' car.

He just took it for a joyride, Michael thought.

"It was a misunderstanding. It's all behind me now."

Michael and Carl talked for a little longer, then Carl left. He hadn't really told Carl anything about his situation, and he was glad.

ASHLEY'S CURIOUS

I have ninety-six dollars. Michael took the bills he'd laid across his bed and put them in an envelope. *I've still got a couple of weeks until prom. I might get two checks from Subway before then.*

He knew it was going to be tight, but he was closer than he'd ever been to getting back to Willmore.

His cell phone rang. It was John.

"I ran into Ashley," John said.

Michael's body went cold. Nobody had brought her up to him in a while.

Nobody from Willmore anyway.

"She asked about you," John went on. "I told her you were in Adlerville, and that you were doing really good. She wanted me to tell you hi."

Relief washed over his body.

She doesn't hate me. She wants to know how I am. She still cares.

He was so excited he could hardly speak. "Should I call her?" he asked.

"She didn't say anything about that. I think she's single now."

John's words were almost everything Michael wanted to hear.

They talked for a little while longer— not about Ashley. They discussed prom plans mainly, but Michael had already mentally checked out. When they got off the phone, he was so overcome with emotion. Tears welled up in his eyes.

This really was all meant to be.

He went over to a mirror that was

hanging on the wall and looked at himself.

Maybe I was meant to lose everything in order to appreciate what I had. To appreciate Ashley. To not argue with her about stupid things like a Justin Bieber song.

As Michael looked at himself in the mirror, he liked who he saw looking back at him. For the first time in a very long time, he didn't feel destroyed.

SPILLING
THE BEANS

So how's everything going?" Mrs. Sefer asked Michael as she checked his bag. "You think you'll be ready for the exit exam?"

"Yeah." Michael wished he could graduate now. He couldn't turn eighteen fast enough. Then he could go back to Porterville.

"Do you still think about Ashley?"

"Yeah," Michael said. He was surprised by the directness of her question. Still, he knew he could talk to Mrs. Sefer.

"I think about her a lot."

"Do you think about seeing her? Like maybe running into her when you're home for the weekend?"

"Sometimes."

Michael decided to tell Mrs. Sefer his plan about going to Willmore's prom. He told her that Ashley had been asking about him.

"Do you think it's good for you to go there? To see her?"

"I want to show Ashley—I want to show everybody—that I'm okay. That I can be calm. That I'm not the person they think I am. I just want to be friends with her."

"I can understand that." Mrs. Sefer smiled slightly. "What if she's just curious? What if she doesn't want a friendship with you? Are you prepared to accept that?"

Michael thought about that question. He felt like he was making progress. That things were slowly going back to how they had been.

"I'd have to accept it," he said.

Mrs. Sefer nodded her head and handed Michael back his bag. This was the first time in a while that he felt like he had given somebody an honest answer—and it was the answer they wanted to hear.

HOME

Jason got promoted at his job," Michael's mom was saying. "He's gonna be making more money. Erik brought his kids here last weekend. They're so funny. They're really into this new game, Minecare or Minecraft or something."

Michael had gone home that weekend. He was in the kitchen doing the dishes with his mom.

She just talks to me like she always has, he told himself. *I think she wants to act like nothing ever happened, but I know she wants to know why I did what I did. She's too scared to ask.*

After Michael finished the dishes, he saw his dad in the living room watching TV. It was a golf tournament.

"Hi, Dad," Michael offered.

Michael knew that if he was really going to get better, he needed to work on his relationship with his dad. As with Ashley, he needed to know that his father wasn't holding what happened at Willmore High School against him.

"Hey, Michael." His father didn't take his eyes off the TV.

Michael watched his dad staring at the screen. He's eyes would close slightly, like he was drowsy, then they'd pop open.

"How's work?" Michael asked. "Is the call center still as busy as ever?"

"Yeah." His father adjusted himself in his chair. "It is. As busy as ever."

"Are you still selling—"

"Michael." His dad's tone was curt, and his eyes were wide open now. "I have to be at that damn place sixty hours a week. I'd rather not talk about it when I'm at home trying to relax."

"Okay."

Michael walked around the house and looked at the pictures of his family. As he did, he noticed something he never had before. In all of the pictures, from when he was young up until a few years ago, Michael was always standing a little bit to the side—away from his family.

He felt his breathing slow a bit.

The more I stare at these pictures, the harder it is for me to breathe.

Michael then found himself in the doorway of his father's study. He stared at the empty gun case.

My dad probably sees this every day, and it reminds him of how disappointed he is with me.

Michael knew these thoughts were not

the right ones to be having. As usual, he couldn't help going to the negative.

It's almost like he's leaving the empty gun case up, hoping that they'll be returned. The only thing that came back was me ... but I think he'd rather have the guns.

MIX

Michael sat at his desktop computer working on a mix CD. Even though his parents had changed around his bedroom, they'd left his computer alone.

He hoped to give it to Ashley at prom.

As the song "Night By Night" by Steely Dan played, Michael realized how much he missed listening to his music. For some reason he hadn't taken his computer to his grandma's house. Since he did all of his schoolwork at Savage, he hadn't really needed it. There weren't many people who wanted to communicate with him, so it wasn't like he was sending a lot of e-mails.

So far the mix had ten tracks.

Give her fifteen. Maybe twenty, he thought to himself as he went through his library of music.

His cell phone rang. He saw that it was John.

"What's up?" Michael asked.

He decided to put the song "Miracles" by Jefferson Starship on the CD. Michael dragged it over into his iTunes playlist.

"You wanna go eat?" John asked.

"Sure," Michael said.

They agreed to meet at Hugo's. It was a Mexican restaurant that Michael used to go to with all the guys.

"So yeah," John went on. They were eating nachos at Hugo's. Michael could tell that John was uncomfortable. He'd even seemed that way even on the phone. "They said you can't come to prom."

"But it's in two weeks." Michael's

stomach was starting to hurt. He felt himself getting cold inside. "Why can't I come?"

"I told you, it had to be cool with the school. Don't you remember?"

"You said it was." Michael was trying not to get angry. He wanted so badly to control himself. For the most part, he'd been doing such a good job at not letting things get to him.

"Kevin and I thought it was. I was called into the principal's office on Thursday. Principal Licea told me you couldn't come. He said the school would be calling your parents. But I got the feeling you didn't know about it when I called. No one told you yet?"

"Maybe they did call my parents," Michael stated bitterly. "They were probably too scared to tell me. Bet they were going to wait until right before I was going to leave to tell me I couldn't go."

"Maybe," John said. He looked slightly relieved.

"I should've known this was going to happen," Michael said in a disgusted voice.

He felt his breathing pick up.

Stay calm. You can work this out, he repeated to himself.

Maybe he had been too open about his plan. Maybe he should have kept it to himself.

"I shouldn't have said anything to anybody. I should have just done it. I jinxed myself," he said.

John stared at him. He didn't know what to say.

"I'm glad you told me," Michael said. "At least you're on my side."

"Yeah, Michael." John took a sip of his Coke. "I am."

Neither of them really touched their food after that.

NEW DAWN
FADES

That Sunday, Michael's parents dropped him off at the bus station. They never stayed with him until the bus came.

They always offer, and I tell them they don't have to. They seem relieved.

Today, they didn't even ask.

They just said good-bye and took off. I don't care. Everybody just takes me for granted. They don't think I care about anything. That's not true! I care most of all.

Michael felt some tears come down his face. All those months of holding everything in—it was getting harder and harder to stay in control. He buried his face in his hoodie and hoped nobody at the station would notice him.

No matter what happens, my plans get messed up. I just have to accept it.

Michael didn't cry too much and eventually lifted up his head. Then he realized his bus was boarding. He grabbed his bag and got on, taking a seat near the back. He put his bag on the seat next to him, hoping nobody would sit there.

I'm not gonna let my plans get messed up anymore. I'm gonna go to prom. People might be mad at first, but they'll forget all about it once they see that I'm okay.

As Michael stared at the road through the bus window, he realized this was the only plan that made sense.

FULL-CIRCLE STOP

It was the Saturday of the Willmore prom.

Michael was in his room at his grand-ma's. He put the rented tuxedo in a gro-cery bag. It had dropped his savings from $187 to seventy-six dollars, but he figured the tuxedo was the most important.

He folded up the bag, covered it with his hoodie, and walked out into the living room. Michael saw the keys to his grand-ma's car hanging up on the hook in the kitchen. She was napping in her bedroom.

Dave came into the kitchen from

the yard and grabbed the keys. He gave Michael a look.

"Dude, you look all neat. What's up?" Dave eyed Michael like he knew Michael wanted the car keys.

"Nothing. Are you taking the car?" Michael had never asked to use it. He hoped he didn't look too suspicious.

"Yeah, mine's in the shop. Did you want to take it somewhere?"

"I was gonna go to the store."

"Why not walk? It's down the street."

"I wanted to practice my driving." Michael thought he sounded convincing.

"I'll drive you. I gotta pick up some stuff anyway. You can drive back if you want." Dave gave him a hard stare. "Cool?"

"Yeah."

As they walked out of the kitchen, Michael discretely took his grandma's spare car keys out of the drawer.

GIMME
SHELTER

Dave and Michael drove to the market near the house. They walked in, and Dave went over to the cereal aisle. Michael acted like he was looking at some magazines in the front.

Now! he told himself. *You have to go now.*

Michael felt himself starting to shake. He turned and started walking. In seconds, he was out of the market. He took out his grandma's spare keys, opened the driver's-side door, and quickly got inside. He put on his seat belt and turned the engine over. Without looking behind him, Michael pulled the car out of the parking spot and drove away.

The freeway on-ramp was close-by. In minutes, Michael was heading east toward Willmore.

He felt sick to his stomach. That familiar cold feeling took over his body. Michael looked at his hands on the steering wheel; they were shaking.

This isn't right. This doesn't feel good at all. It's too much like that morning at Willmore with the gun.

Before, he had been so fixated on Ashley that he didn't mind feeling that way if he thought it would somehow get them back together. But Michael had been trying to work on himself, and suddenly he wondered if maybe this whole plan was a step backward.

For a split second, he thought about

turning around. Nobody was expecting him to show up at the prom. He wasn't supposed to go anyway. He wouldn't be disappointing anyone if he didn't show up.

Except myself.

He could still turn around.

What will I tell Dave? How will I explain taking the car?

As Michael passed more exits, he realized he wasn't going to stop driving to Willmore.

I have to go, he realized.

He was trying to quiet the voice in his head that was urging him to turn around.

QUICK
CHANGE

The Willmore prom was being held at the Lakewood Country Club, which was in the richest part of town. Michael had driven around here before with his parents.

Before he got too close, he pulled into a strip mall and went into an Island's Restaurant to change.

The place was packed with families out for a meal on Saturday night. Michael walked directly into the restroom and into the largest stall it had. As he put on the tuxedo, he heard people come in and out.

Once he was finished getting dressed, he waited until there was nobody in the restroom. As he closed up the grocery bag with his regular clothes in it, he realized Ashley's mix CD was still in the bag.

He fished it out. He'd written her name across the front in black marker. He tucked it away in the pocket of his tuxedo jacket.

As he stepped out of the stall, he went over to the mirror to check himself out. He straightened his clip-on bow tie, made sure his shirt didn't looked bunched up, and adjusted his pants at the waist.

You look good, Michael, he told himself. *You could've gotten a haircut, but other than that you look fine.*

He grabbed the bag with his street clothes and walked out of the restroom.

MY OLD
SCHOOL

Michael pulled into the parking lot of the country club. He followed a long winding road lined with shady trees, which led up to the main building where the dance was being held.

Michael quickly realized the only way to park was to valet his car. He hadn't had a lot of experience driving, let alone valet parking.

I don't like this. I don't want to give them my keys.

Michael stopped in front of the valets.

They walked over to his car and opened the driver's-side door.

"Welcome to Lakewood Country Club, sir." The valet was older than Michael.

Michael got out of the car. The valet handed him a ticket.

Then the valet took Michael's car and drove off.

He took it like I'm just another person from Willmore. Nobody really knows that I'm not supposed to be here.

Michael looked at the ticket. It said "Lakewood Country Club" on it. It also had a number.

"I get my car back with this?" Michael asked another valet, who was texting on his phone. He stood next to a small stand. On it were a bunch of hooks with keys hanging from them.

"Yeah, when you're ready to leave," the valet said.

Michael took deep breath and walked

into the club.

He knew coming here was a huge mistake the minute he walked into the dance.

The prom was in a big hall. The decorations were dazzling. He'd never seen anything like it. Everything was bright and white and twinkling. There were students sitting at tables, dancing, and taking photos. The DJ was blasting "Teach Me How to Dougie."

There are people everywhere. I can barely move through the crowd, and I don't recognize anyone. I haven't been to Willmore in over a year. There's a lot of new people.

For a moment, Michael was frozen. He thought about leaving right then, but he knew he wouldn't.

Calm down, he told himself. *Breathe. Find your friends. Let them see you. Let them know you're here.*

Michael made his way through the

crowd. He felt like everybody was looking at him. Like they knew he shouldn't be there. He continued moving.

I hope Ashley doesn't see me before I see her. He wanted their reunion to happen on his terms.

Eventually, Michael spotted John, Kevin, and some more of their friends from the track team. They were standing near the punch bowl with their dates.

Michael walked up behind John. Everyone looked at him wide-eyed.

They're all so surprised. I've perfected my role as an outcast in their eyes. A weirdo. A loose cannon.

John turned around. He tried to hide how surprised he was when he saw Michael, but he couldn't.

"Michael, uh … " John said.

"Hey." Michael smiled. He was doing his best to act normal. To be the person people remembered him being.

"Dude … " John looked around. "You better bail. If any of the teachers see you, you'll get in a lot of trouble. We both will."

Michael didn't know what to say. He knew John was right. He felt like he'd come so far for nothing.

John just stared at him. The lights from a disco ball illuminated parts of his face as the loud, intrusive music that Michael hated continued to blare.

Michael looked around the hall. That's when he saw Ashley on the dance floor. Michael tried to see who she was dancing with. Whoever it was had his back to him. He continued to watch her move to the music. The twinkling lights of the disco ball surrounded her.

She's so perfect.

Michael's heart was starting to be beat really fast. He felt his stomach starting to hurt. The cold feeling was coming over him like it always did when he thought about her.

She looks like she's having a good time.

He got even colder. It was getting too intense. He started to feel like the walls were closing in, like he couldn't breathe.

This seems to be the only feeling I have whenever I see her.

And at that moment, Michael Bryan Ellis realized something he never thought he would.

He couldn't be around Ashley.

Ever again.

I don't want to feel this way anymore. I can't go back to that. That's not me. That's not what I want my life to be about.

The coldness receded with the realization. But not completely.

It just wasn't as strong. In a strange way, Michael felt like he had some control over it now.

Then the song "Baby" by Justin Bieber came blasting over the speakers. A lot of the students on the dance floor laughed. Some of them cheered.

Ashley did both.

I placed so much importance on her place in my life that I forgot about myself. He looked around at all the Willmore students. They were enjoying the prom just like they were supposed to.

I don't know any of these people anymore. This isn't my school.

"Michael, bro," John started again. "I don't want you to leave, but you're gonna get in big trouble if you don't. They're gonna call the cops if they see you."

Michael didn't even look at him.

He got his bearings and walked toward the door he'd come in from. He thought about taking one last look at Ashley but realized there was no point.

Michael left the Willmore prom.

For the first time in his life, Michael realized he wasn't inadequate. He didn't need to feel unimportant or uncomfortable around the popular crowd. He had something to offer. He didn't need acceptance in order to be himself.

The only person he'd really been fighting with was him.

SOMEDAY
NEVER COMES

As Michael started his grandma's car, he felt something jabbing at his chest.

Ashley's CD.

He took it out of his jacket and put it in the CD player.

"Coming Back to Me" by Jefferson Airplane came on. It immediately made him sad, but he didn't turn it off.

Why am I going to drive back to my grandma's? Why am I in school to take the exit exam? Why am I doing anything?

Michael was again wallowing in his misery. He couldn't help it.

I have no family, no real friends, and no Ashley.

He felt a lone tear burn as it rolled down his cheek.

"I've wasted so much time!" he screamed out loud.

As the song continued, Michael started to really cry. He was having trouble breathing because he was crying so hard. He should've pulled over, but he couldn't. For some reason he wanted to keep going. He needed to leave Willmore as fast as possible.

And this is all because of that stupid gun I brought to school. I wasn't going to hurt Ashley with it. But nobody believes that. Nobody would listen to me. They still won't.

Thoughts flooded his head. They came fast and furious.

"I was going to kill myself," he managed to say through the tears. Michael was unable to hide from himself any longer. "And I wanted her to see it. I wanted everybody to see it! Then they'd have to deal with me."

Michael pushed eject on the CD player. Then he took Ashley's CD and threw it out the window.

BRINGING
IT DOWN

Michael's parents were finishing up dinner when he walked into the house. They were startled to see him.

He'd composed himself in the car before he'd come in. Seeing his parents, he started crying all over again.

"You took your grandma's car?" his father asked.

"I'm sorry about what happened." Michael was bawling. "I'm sorry I let you both down. I'm sorry about what I did. I'm sorry about everything. I'm … sorry about me."

Michael wrapped his arms around his father. He was breathing heavily, and he felt his father's body stiffen. Was it concern? He buried his face in his father's shoulder.

Michael's dad hugged him back.

"I know you didn't mean it, Michael," his dad said softly into his ear. "I know you didn't mean any of it."

We'll get you the help you need, honey," Michael's mother said. "You're going to be okay."

"You know I love you, son. I love you," his dad said with sincerity.

Michael spent the night at his parents' house. His real home.

They called his grandma to let her know that Michael was there and the car was fine.

As Michael lay down on his bed, his head was swirling. As he stared at the ceiling in the darkness, he felt a strange sensation.

The past is behind me. For better or worse, tonight I went from having everything to prove to having nothing to prove. Not to those people anyway.

Michael liked the way he felt. It was so liberating, no longer feeling that burden. He went to sleep the moment he closed his eyes.

OUT OF STEP

Michael apologized to his grandma and Dave when he got home Sunday afternoon. They told him that it was okay; they understood.

"Just don't do something like that again. You could've gotten in real trouble if we'd called the police," Dave said.

Michael knew it. He also promised he wouldn't do anything like that again.

And he meant it.

Despite feeling like a weight had been lifted, he was very listless that Monday at school. He went through the motions as he did his packets and worked on his

Wuthering Heights report.

At snack time, he saw Carl looking around for him, but Michael stayed away. Carl hadn't been in class earlier, so they didn't get a chance to talk. They were behind on their history project.

I have nothing to tell him about Willmore's prom anyway.

Michael started wandering around the campus and found himself on the field. It was really small. There were bleachers sitting randomly in the middle. He walked over to them and sat down on the top row.

The view wasn't anything special, just the rooftops of houses.

Michael just sat there waiting for the bell to ring.

I've got nothing on my mind, he realized. *Except my future. What happens after I graduate? Will I go to community college in Willmore? Somewhere else? Here maybe? Do I still want to be a doctor?*

He hadn't thought about his future in a long time.

I haven't been able to think about anything else but Ashley and Willmore High. Now that's gone.

"How's the view up there?" Mrs. Sefer called to him.

Michael turned around and saw her standing behind the bleachers.

"Mind if I sit with you?" she asked.

"Not at all." Michael smiled. He liked that Mrs. Sefer cared about him.

They talked for a little while. She asked about his weekend. He didn't feel like talking about Willmore. She didn't ask any questions about it.

"You know, Mrs. Sefer, I don't have anything on my mind right now," Michael eventually said. "Just my future."

"How does that feel? To be focused on that."

"It's scary."

"I think you're going to be just fine." Mrs. Sefer smiled.

"I hope I am," he replied.

"You will be," she continued. "I think you know that too."

The bell rang.

"I have to get back to class."

Michael stood up and walked down the bleachers. Mrs. Sefer stayed put.

"You gonna stay out here?" he asked.

"For a few moments more, I suppose. I like the view."

"Really? You're not gonna add anything? No more lectures? No more advice?"

"If you insist. Take advantage of our counseling service while you're here. You might enjoy it." Mrs. Sefer went back to staring at the rooftops.

Michael went back to class.

STILL ON PAROLE

Michael sat in his room reading *Wuthering Heights* as quickly as possible. He liked it. Even though he knew that things might end badly for the main characters, it was interesting seeing their relationship from the outside. He'd also started on his report. Surprisingly, it hadn't been as hard as he thought it would be.

My head is clearing up. I can think a lot easier now. I feel kind of like my old self. He was happy about that.

The doorbell rang.

Since nobody ever came to visit him here, he didn't get up to get it.

The doorbell rang again.

He was so into his book he didn't realize his grandma had left the house. He sighed and got up to answer the door.

"Good evening, Michael," Allen, his parole officer, said when he opened the door.

"Hi," Michael said nervously. "Is there something wrong?"

Someone saw me at the prom. They reported me. I wasn't supposed to be there.

"Nothing's wrong." Allen smiled. "Just making my monthly rounds. You mind if I come in?"

"No." Michael moved out of the doorway, allowing Allen inside.

Before Michael could start getting angry, he realized he didn't need to be. He was on the right track now. He believed what Mrs. Sefer said: "You're going to be just fine."

Allen looked around a little bit. But he didn't lift up any cushions on the couch or touch anything.

"How's school?"

"Good. I'm actually working on a report for English right now."

"That's great."

"I'm going to be taking the exit exam. I'm going to graduate. Then I'm going to community college."

"Here or Willmore?"

"I don't know."

Michael hated saying that, but it was the truth.

"Well," Allen's cell phone buzzed, and he looked to see who it was. "It looks like you've gone from being a model ward to a model parolee."

He didn't stay long after that. He shook Michael's hand, took one last look around, and then he was gone.

Michael walked back to his room. He wanted to finish *Wuthering Heights*.

He wanted to know how the story ended.

As he was getting ready for bed, his cell phone rang. It was John—Michael's link to Willmore and the past.

He picked up the phone, letting it vibrate in his hand.

Michael let the call go to voice mail.

STAYING ON TRACK

"So what happened last weekend?" Carl asked when he and Michael were eating. "At your old school?"

"I got there and realized I didn't care about those people anymore, so I left." Michael knew there was more to tell, but he felt good telling the story that way. It was the truth.

"What?" Carl almost coughed out the muffin he was eating. "But you had all those plans."

"Yeah," Michael started. "I just realized

I had more important things to do than focus on my past."

"Didn't you want to show them they didn't end you? That they couldn't push you around?"

"Maybe I showed them that by not caring about them anymore." As Michael said the words, he realized they made sense.

"Maybe," said Carl. He shrugged. "Did you finish the history packet? I'm stuck on this one part."

"Let's go back to class. I wanna work on my *Wuthering Heights* report anyway. We can look at your packet. Plus, we need to work on our history project."

They got up and went back to class.

JENNIFER

During English class, Michael printed out the first draft of his *Wuthering Heights* book report. Then the teacher partnered him up with a girl named Jennifer because they were reading the same book.

Her hair's so blonde, Michael thought. *Like shiny blonde. It makes her look special.*

"It's just a first draft," Jennifer said. "So be nice if it sucks."

"So is mine," Michael responded.

He started to read her draft. Right away he could tell that she had missed a few key points of the story.

She doesn't seem to understand the

characters. Why it's so hard for them to not be together. I can't tell her that, though. She'll have to redo the whole report.

"Yours is really good," Jennifer said. "You made way better points than I did."

"Thanks." Michael smiled sheepishly. "Yours is good too."

"You lie." Jennifer's face was blank. "I didn't read the whole book. I didn't have time. I just know it's about these people who have an obsessive relationship."

"Yeah." Michael was trying not to sound like a know-it-all. "They want to be together, but they can't be."

"I kinda got that. I looked up some stuff on the Internet, but my brain's so scattered."

"Mine is too. I'm almost done with the book, but I have to really concentrate when I read it."

"What do you think of it?" Jennifer

stared at him in just the same way Ashley did.

"I like it. But in real life it's better to not be with someone if they're no good for you."

"Like my ex-boyfriend. He's a total loser."

They talked for a little while longer, then it was time to go.

As Michael packed up his things, he watched Jennifer leave the classroom. She waved to him as she left.

NEW DIRECTION

Michael folded his graded *Wuthering Heights* report in half as he walked to the snack area. He'd gotten an A-minus.

As he walked, he looked around at all the other students. They talked with one another. They browsed their phones. Some sat alone. Each had a story.

We're all at Savage because we made mistakes. Now we need to learn from them and make our lives better.

He spotted Carl. They had to finish their history report. Once they connected and made a plan, Michael headed to his grandma's to study. He wasn't scheduled to work at Subway that day.

While he was walking home, he realized that he was going to be continually thrust into many situations. He would confront different levels of uncertainty. That's what living was about. Nothing was going to be perfect. But there would be moments of perfection. And peace.

I'm going to have to work harder than most, but I know deep down I can deal with it.

He finally grasped that everything he thought his life was about—Ashley, Willmore—was all in his head.

That's why it was so hard for me to let go of everything. If I didn't give up my past, I wouldn't be where I am now. Having a new life. Having to face myself. I guess I wasn't ready to look in the mirror.

Now that his life was no longer about

the past, his head was not filled with pre-conceived ideas of what people thought about him or how they would treat him.

My life's a blank slate now. I can just be myself.

The weather was crisp, perfect for running. Even though there was a spring chill, which usually reminded him of the time when he and Ashley first met, Michael Bryan Ellis didn't think about her at all.

Here, Evan is recording a voice for his animated horror film, Insect.

ABOUT THE AUTHOR

Evan Jacobs was born in Long Island, New York. His family moved to California when he was four years old. They settled in Fountain Valley, where he still lives today.

As a filmmaker, Evan has directed eleven low-budget films. He has also had various screenplays produced and realized by other directors. He co-wrote the film *Knockout*, starring "Stone Cold" Steve Austin. He co-authored the thriller *Distant Shore*. He is currently juggling several movie and book projects.

Evan is also a behavior interventionist for people who have special needs. He works with a variety of students to make their days as successful as possible. His third young adult novel, *Screaming Quietly*, won a Moonbeam Children's Book Award bronze medal. You can find out more about him at www.anhedeniafilms.blogspot.com.